LOCKED DOWN BY HOOD LOVE

BY LATOYA NICOLE

DEDICATION

To my daughter. I remember when I sat in front of the doctors when you were three years old and they told me that you were on the spectrum. Immediately, I began to cry. It hurt my heart that it was another battle you had to fight. You had already been through so much, and I couldn't stop the tears from falling. That was until I knew what that meant. I had no idea I was getting a beautiful, very smart, funny, different, and loving child. You have brought me so much joy and I can honestly say you changed me for the better. You are my everything and you will never have to wonder if anyone loves you. I will make sure that you are overflowed with love. You're my heartbeat and I'm blessed to have you. Keep being you and never stop standing out. I LOVE YOU MIRACLE MONÉT RILEY

Acknowledgements

IT'S SO MANY PEOPLE I WANT TO THANK, I OFTEN FORGET. JUST KNOW THAT I LOVE YOU ALL AND I'M GRATEFUL FOR EVERYTHING THAT EVERYONE DOES FOR ME. THE LOVE AND SUPPORT YOU AL GIVE ME IS SIMPLY AMAZING. MY READERS NEVER LET ME DOWN AND I JUST WANT YOU ALL TO KNOW I APPRECIATE YOU FROM THE BOTTOM OF MY HEART.

HAPPY BDAY TO SARAI. I HOPE YOU SPEND ALL YOUR MOMMY'S MONEY AND GET EVERYTHING YOUR HEART DESIRES. DON'T LET KIMMIE TELL YOU SHE BROKE.

HAPPY 21ST BDAY JADA BLACK YOU GROWN NOW BABY MAMA I LOVE YOU I HOPE YOU ENJOY YOUR DAY

HAPPY BDAY TO MY COUSIN CHRIS I KNOW YOU'RE SERVING OUR COUNTRY, BUT I HOPE YOU TAKE THE TIME TO ENJOY YOUR DAY I LOVE YOU.

TO MY PUBLISHER, THANK YOU FOR EVERYTHING THAT YOU DO FOR ME. I APPRECIATE ALL OF YOUR SUPPORT AND ALL THE THINGS YOU HAVE INSTILLED IN ME. KEEP BEING YOU AND KEEP PUSHING FORWARD.

TO MY MLPP FAMILY I LOVE YOU GUYS AND OUR TIME IS HERE. DON'T GIVE UP AND ALWAYS AIM HIGH. I LOVE YOU.

TO MY BESTIE, GIRL YOU KNOW I I I LOVE YOU. NO MATTER WHAT YOU DO. LOL THANK YOU BOO FOR BEING THERE FOR ME. I APPRECIATE YOU AND ALL OF OUR TALKS. YOU ARE AMAZING AND I'M GLAD I FOUND SOMEONE LIKE YOU. TELL DONOVAN TWO TO THE FACE IF HE KEEPS PLAYING WITH ME.

TO MY BAE ZATASHA AKA ZEE BAE I'M SO PROUD OF YOU AND ALL THE THINGS YOU ARE ACCOMPLISHING. NEVER LET ANYONE STEAL YOUR DREAMS. THANK YOU FOR ALWAYS BEING THERE FOR ME NO MATTER WHAT. YOU ARE TRULY AMAZING, AND I LOVE YOU.

KRISSY HEY MY OLD BOO. I LOVE YOU AND THANK YOU FOR KEEPING ME ON MY TOES. YOU ARE THE REASON I HAVE TO BE ON POINT. YOU HAVE A GREAT SPIRIT AND I APPRECIATE YOU.

KB COLE I LOVE YOU EVEN THOUGH YOUR ASS BE ACTING FUNNY NOW. YOU ARE MY SISTER FOR LIFE AND I LOVE YOU. KEEP PUSHING OUT THOSE DOPE ASS BOOKS. YOU'RE AN AMAZING PERSON AND I APPRECIATE YOU.

TO MY AMAZING COUSIN, I LOVE YOU SO MUCH AND I DON'T KNOW WHAT I WOULD DO WITHOUT YOUR ASS SOME DAYS. YOU ARE THE SHIT AND I HOPE YOU CHANGE YOUR MIND. YOU ARE A DOPE ASS WRITER, AND EVERYONE NEEDS TO READ YOUR WORK. IF YOU HAVEN'T CHECKED HER OUT, PLEASE DO SO. AJ DAVIDSON YOU ARE AMAZING DON'T PUT DOWN YOUR PEN.

PANDA I LOVE YOU BOO MAKE SURE YALL GO CHECK OUT HER BOOKS. SHE HAS THE URBAN ROMANCE ON LOCK. KEEP MOVING TOWARDS YOUR GOAL ITS COMING.

BLAKE KARRINGTON THANK YOU FOR EVERYTHING YOU'RE A DOPE AUTHOR AND FRIEND I APPRECIATE YOU YALL GO CHECK

OUT HIS CATALOG AND JOIN HIS READING GROUP FOR READERS

ONLY.

THANK YOU TO EVERYONE THAT DOWNLOADED THIS

BOOK. BEWARE IT IS FILLED WITH DRAMA, LOVE, SEX, AND PETTY

LOL I'M GOING IN HIDING ONCE YOU ALL START DOWNLOADING.

SPECIAL THANK YOU TO SHVONNE LATRICE FOR

ALLOWING ME TO USE HER AS A CHARACTER VISUAL AND

CHARACTER FOR THIS BOOK. I APPRECIATE YOU AND THANK YOU

FROM THE BOTTOM OF MY HEART.

CHAPTER ONE SHVONNE

"Go best friend that's my best friend. You better ohhh you better." Bending over, I twerked like I was getting paid for it as my best friend Tiana egged me on. I may have been thin, but I could move what I had. A bitch could throw that ass with them big booty bitches. "Damn Pebbles, your ass ain't tired yet? My big ass is wore out." Laughing, I turned the music down and poured us a drink. Pebbles is the name my boyfriend gave me. They called him Bam Bam and he thought it would be cute for me to be called Pebbles. Somehow, it just stuck.

"You're so damn extra. Your ass twenty pounds bigger than me and your ass acting like you about to die. All you were doing was playing DJ. Your ass ain't bust one move, but over here breathing like you done ran a marathon."

"Fuck you. Where we at with it tonight. A bitch trying to hit the club." Looking at her like she was crazy, I couldn't do anything but laugh.

"How the hell you trying to turn up, but you just turned down after hitting next on the radio? Besides, me and Bam got some shit to do. You know the business never stops." The sad look crossed her face, but she knew how we got down. If he banging, I'm busting.

"Why you won't put me on? I'm tired of working in the bank, I'm ready to rob that mother fucker. If shit don't get better soon, I'm gone be out here selling this thang for a hundred dollars an hour." Laughing, I tried to change the subject. I loved her, and she was my best friend, but baby girl wasn't about this life. How could I live with myself if something happened to her?

"We can go out tomorrow. I'll get the crew to go so your ass can find a man. Let one of these niggas pay your bills. I can't have my best friend out here turning tricks for some Trix. I'm gone call your ass Trixie." My phone rung, and I was happy this conversation was ending.

"Hey ma, what you and T over there doing?" Everything about Bam turned me on. I was ready to leave and go fuck right now just from his voice.

"Shit, just booling. I'll be home in a little while. What time are we heading out?" Bloods hate to say words with the letter C, so I was always joking around with him.

"After I get some pussy. Meet me there in about twenty minutes." Not even waiting for me to answer, Bam hung up the phone and I turned towards Tiana. I knew her ass was about to be pissed, but fuck that. It's not my fault she didn't have a man. I had one and as long as I did, when he called I was coming. It's been three years since me and Bam started dating and nobody could tell me shit. My baby was fine as hell and all the bitches wanted him. Six feet, deep chocolate and a body sent from the Gods.

His looks weren't the only thing they were after. My baby was a Blood and he ran these streets in Los Angeles. Everybody knew not to fuck with him or his crew and that included me. It's like I was queen out here and I loved that shit. We lived a good life and I wouldn't trade that shit for nothing in the world. His

family was killed by some Crips and mine died in a car crash when

I was younger. It was only him, his brother, mother and father.

They died in a house fire. If he wasn't out in the streets hustling,

he would have been there as well. When my grandmother passed

away a year ago, me and Bam moved in together. We were all

each other had and that drew us closer together.

"Best friend, I'm about to get out of here. I promise we will

go out tomorrow. Your ass better kill it too. If you come out that

door looking a mess, bitch I'm pulling off."

"When have I ever dressed fucked up?" She tried it, but

her ass will throw some bullshit together in a minute. Everybody

know my clothes and shoe game is nice, so I need everyone

around me to be on point.

"Let's end this conversation before I hurt your feelings. Be

on point or stay your ass here. Send pics first if you have to. I'll call

you later." Walking out the door, I jumped in my white on white

Benz. I called my bitch Snow and I loved her ass. It was my

LOCKED DOWN BY HOOD LOVE   LATOYA NICOLE

birthday gift from Bam and it still smelled like the show room. My

text went off and I saw it was Tiana.

BEST FRIEND: Now wtf I'm supposed to do since you

gone? A bitch sitting here looking at the fucking wall.

ME: Go grab your bullet and use pulse number seven

BEST FRIEND: Fuck you bitch

ME: You wish, but I'm about to go fuck this long dick.

Placing my phone back in my MCM bag, I didn't even wait

for her respond. Everyone always got mad at me and Bam. They

say it's unhealthy for two people to be that close. Me and Bam

grew up in the same neighborhood. We were like best friends and

even back then we were inseparable. I've always been drawn to

the bloods; bad boys were my thing. Give me a rough neck with

some tats and a beard any day. All the way home, I smiled at the

first time we met. Bam wasn't fine back then, but his rough ass

demeanor made all the girls want him.

Walking through the hall, I wanted to see what the hell

was going on. It was a crowd of people screaming and hollering.

11

Pushing my way through, I made it to the front and Bam was beating the shit out of a Freshman. He had hands and that's how he actually got his name. I've never seen someone get hit so many times in one minute in all my life. Reaching in the guy's pocket, Bam took his money. Standing there counting it, his ass started talking shit.

"The next time I have to lay hands on you for my money, you won't get your ass back up. Bitch ass nigga." Before I could shoot my shot, a girl walked up and tried to leave with Bam.

"Baby where we headed?" The way she said it, her ass may as well have said can I suck your dick. His ass never looked up when he responded.

"You heading to the cafeteria I'm sure." Giving a fake laugh, she grabbed his arm still choosing.

"I'm Muffin. Let's get out of here and I can show you why I have that name." Trying not to laugh, I couldn't wait for his response.

"Look biscuit. Is it biscuit? You got about five seconds to get the fuck away from me or I'm going to knock piss out your ass." This bitch was still about to shoot her shot, until I walked up and punched her ass dead in the mouth.

"Get the fuck out of my man's face." Embarrassed, she ran off and Bam shook his head. My ass just knew I was in there until he spoke.

"Your ass crazy. Thank you ma, but your skinny ass ain't my type either. You can be on my team though." That nigga treated the shit out of my ass, but after that we hung every day. Whenever he had issues with a bitch, he would have me beat they ass. It went on like that until I graduated. Right after I walked across the stage, he took me home and fucked the shit out of me.

Mother fuckers could hate if they wanted to, but it was Pebbles and Bam Bam for life.

CHAPTER TWO BAM

Standing outside my homies studio, me and the crew played a few dice games. If it wasn't shit else for us to do, our ass would be out here for hours until somebody got tired. My ass never stayed out here long because I would rather be under Pebbles. Since I was the only nigga that had a girl, they made sure they clowned me on the shit every chance they got. It would bother me if it was anybody but my chick.

She was just like one of the guys. I trained her ass that way. Her ass been up under me since she was fifteen and I was able to mold her ass. I'll trust her with my life over any one of these niggas. My girl was a ridah and it didn't bother me hanging out with her ass. We were on the come up, and all these niggas wanted to do was fuck off their money. Me and Pebbles had dreams to run these streets.

The only thing I didn't like was how she brought out the worse in me. See, my girl was fine as hell and it always prompted

14

some dumb ass nigga to come at her. My bitch was so fine, a nigga would come at her while I was standing there, and shit never ended well for their ass. A nigga was out here trying to get money, not killing niggas over something that was already mine.

At one point, she was just Shvonne to everybody else. The first time I laid eyes on her, I knew she was gone be my bitch. I had to let her young ass marinate though. My lifestyle was too much for her at the time. I needed to make sure she could handle that shit. I'll never tell her, but my dick was hard as hell the first time I saw her.

Before her, I always had a type. A big booty thick chocolate bitch. She was the exact opposite. High yellow, petite, with long ass curly hair. Even though she wasn't my type, it was no denying how pretty she was. My bitch was bad, and she was all mine. I'll kill a nigga dead over that one and I didn't give a fuck who thought the shit was lame. When you find a bitch that can accept you for who you are and not try to change you, she's a keeper.

15

As soon as these niggas started arguing, I knew it was time for me to get the fuck out of here. Why the fuck I wanted to sit here and listen to these niggas bitch, and I could be at home in some pussy.

"You niggas can have this shit, I'm out." You could hear they gay asses smacking and shit.

"We already knew the shit was coming. Gone take your sprung ass home. I'm surprised you made it this far, didn't know her leash could come all the way over here." Everybody laughed at Jim, but I didn't find shit funny.

"Bitch my dick is the leash. Don't get mad at me your shit ain't long enough for her to make it to the dresser. Nigga got finger food for a dick." All he could do was look stupid while everyone laughed. Everybody knew that nigga was lacking. This bitch named Kelly told anyone who would listen how she had to hold the shit with two fingers to suck it.

"We'll holla at your sprung ass tomorrow. I'm about to get out of here myself. I'm trying to find some pussy to get into tonight." Lick thought he slid out of the shit, but I was about to light his ass up too.

"You need to slide your ass to the clinic. Don't think we don't know your ass fucked Faith and everybody know that bitch burning. Need to go get treated. Issa leaky." I had to laugh at me using the shit Pebbles ass be saying. The shit do be funny as fuck even though I don't know what the shit means. Fuck is a damn issa?

Not giving them a chance to respond, I walked off and jumped in my Lexus truck. I was able to buy my girl a car, but I wanted to give her the world. We had money, but I wanted it all. No matter what we had to do, or who we had to cross to get it, I wanted it. I've already made a name for myself, so mother fuckers knew not to fuck with me. Basically, a young nigga did what the fuck he wanted to do, and it wouldn't be long before I ran all this shit.

Pulling into our condo, I couldn't wait to get in the house. I've been outside all day preparing for this hit me and Pebbles had on tomorrow. It was gone set us up for a while, but that didn't mean we was stopping.

When I walked in the door, my girl was grinding on a stripper pole trying to be sexy and shit. I swear she was just like a nigga, but I loved the fact that she was still girly. It ain't like she had to try hard, all she had to do was stand still. Instead, her ass was swinging around in the front room trying to imitate a stripper. My ass was trying not to laugh, but the shit had me in tears.

"Pebbles what the fuck you doing? You know your ass can't dance." My dick was hard as fuck. I always told her she couldn't dance because I didn't want her to be doing that shit for another nigga. When she saw I was getting excited, her ass stuck her tongue out and got cocky. Jumping back on the pole, she tried to slide down and bust her shit. I tried to contain my laughter, but the pained look on her face made me lose my shit.

"Fuck you Bam. Your bitch ass ain't have to laugh. I done hurt my whole left side. Can't never be serious for shit. Help me up." Laughing so hard it was tears in my eyes, I walked right past

18

her. Kicking her in the knee on my way by, I almost passed out when she grunted. All that shit she was talking, hell naw I wasn't helping her up.

"I know your tough ass not acting like a free sissy. Get your sensitive ass in here and come get this dick. You worried about that lil ass bump you got from falling. Worry about what this dick about to do to your cervix." Knowing she couldn't turn down good dick, I laughed as I watched her limp with one heel on to the room.

"Bet I don't try to do nothing else sexy for your ass. Move out the way." Slapping me on my arm, she headed to the room. I loved when she was pissed. This was about to be some good aggressive sex. When I walked in the room, she was laying in the bed looking sad and shit. Softening up, I climbed on top of her.

Kissing her softly on shoulder, I moved her curls out of her face. She was so fucking fine, sometimes I couldn't believe a nigga like me got her. Working my way down to her nipples, I loved the way they sat up all pretty and perfect.

19

"You love me girl?" Even though she tried to fight it, her body was giving in like a mother fucker. Soft moans escaped her mouth and I knew then she was just playing mad.

"Hurry up and put it in shit." Laughing, I gave her exactly what she wanted. I've been trying to get her ass pregnant. The way I'm feeling, tonight might be the night. Releasing my aching dick, I got ready to fuck her stupid.

CHAPTER 3 SHVONNE

Me and Bam been out robbing niggas all day, and we made a decent profit. Even though they were scared of Bam, they would try to kill us if they knew it was us hitting their stash spots. Our ass was into everything, whatever it took to get that cash. My man was going to make sure we were going to make it and I trusted him with my life.

"Pebbles, I'm about to go hang out with my niggas. Don't be late and shit coming to the club. You know how you get when your ass trying to figure out what to wear." His ass was always complaining about how long it took me to get ready but be all over me when once I'm dressed.

"Shut the fuck up. I'll be there you just make sure you keep them bitches out of your face. Don't make me beat a bitch in the temple with my Chanels. Try me if you want to." Laughing, the nigga walked off from me like I wasn't dead ass serious.

"Stop playing with me. Don't get your lil ass knocked out in that bitch. You know I don't play that tough shit in public. If you wanna beat something, beat this dick. Be on time." Throwing my shoe at him, I was pissed when it hit the wall. As soon as he left, I called my best friend to come get me. When I told her why I wanted her to come, she damn near flew out the door.

Grabbing my wallet, I waited for Tiana to pull up. My ass been sick for the past few days, and I needed to get a test.

BEST FRIEND: I'm outside bitch!!!

ME: On the way out

Grabbing what I needed, I headed out the door and jumped in the car. This bitch was more excited than I was.

"I'm about to be an auntie bitch." I don't think she could do anything without sticking her tongue out and attempting to twerk.

"We don't know yet. Let's go bitch so we're not late tonight. Bam gone kick my ass and if he beat me, bitch I'm beating you. Issa slap party."

22

"Girl shut the fuck up, the damn Walgreens is five minutes away. It takes five minutes to piss how the fuck you gone be late. Always gotta be extra."

"Just drive." Pulling into the parking lot, I ran in and got the test. On the way home, it's like both of us were deep in thought. It was quiet as hell. As soon as the car stopped, I ran inside to the bathroom. My ass was nervous as fuck as I laid the test on the sink. It was the longest five minutes of my life. When the five minutes were up, I looked at the stick and couldn't control my crying.

"I knew I was about to be an auntie. I'm so happy for you guys. When are you going to tell him?" Knowing the club was not the place for it, I decided to wait until later tonight.

"When we get back from the club. Let's get dressed before we have to fight that nigga for real."

Our ass rushed and got dressed and we were out the door in an hour. I couldn't believe I was about to be a mom. I couldn't wait to tell Bam, his ass was going to go crazy. His ass been trying to get me pregnant since we been together. This was what we have been saving for and now it was finally here. Rubbing my hand over my belly, it took everything in me not to start crying again.

"Bitch pull yourself together. Your ass in here about to do the ugly cry before we walk in the damn club. I promise you I'm not walking in with Ceily. You got me fucked up." Laughing, I tried to pull myself together.

"Okay, I'm ready." Heading inside, we looked around until we spotted Bam. Him and the crew already had a section and walked over to it. Tiana didn't waste any time turning up. Sitting on Bam's lap, I watched her laughing. It was the perfect night, and it was going to end just as perfect.

Everything was going fine until some guys walked in the club and tried to come in our section. You could tell they weren't from here or they would have known this shit was off limits.

"Hey nigga you drunk or something. Where the fuck you from? I know you gotta be from out of town pulling some shit like this." The guy looked at him like he was dirt beneath his shoes.

After telling him where he was from, Bam wouldn't let the shit go.

My gut told me shit was about to go left and I tried my best to

calm it down.

"It's fine baby, let's just enjoy our night." Bam was about

to let it go until dude spoke again.

"Listen to your bitch she may just save your life." This

nigga was cocky as fuck, but I know Bam and he wasn't about to

let that slide. Before anybody could react to the shit dude said, he

pulled his gun and fired. It's like he knew what was about to

happen and decided to kick it off first. None of us saw that shit

coming and it gave him the upper hand. Everyone was scattering

for cover, but it was too late for Bam. Trying to run towards him, I

got hit with a stray bullet and I went down as well.

You could hear screams and everyone running, but all I

could do was look at Bam. His eyes were open and focused on me,

but I could tell he was already gone. As I faded in and out, I tried

to keep my eyes focused on the love of my life. He was all I had

25

and now he was gone. I never got to tell him about the baby and now it was too late. Maybe if I had told him, we would have gotten out of here and he would be alive. Knowing all I had left of him was the baby, I tried my best to keep my eyes open. The shit hurt and them bitches was heavy.

The guy walked over to Bam and grabbed his face. I wanted to help him, but I couldn't. The guy slammed Bam's head to the ground and walked off. It was the last thing I saw before everything went black.

****

"I need to know if my baby is okay. Please just get me the doctor, I need to make sure my baby is okay."

"Please calm down. The doctor will be in here shortly and explain everything to you. Just please let me take your vitals." Hoping it would get her out of there quicker, I allowed her to do her job. Hearing someone come in the door, I got excited thinking it was the doctor, but it was Tiana. I don't know why but seeing her with just a bandage around her arm pissed me off. It's not like

26

I wanted her to die, but I just didn't understand why Bam had to die. Everyone was alive and well, but he wasn't. You could see the sympathetic look on her face, but that shit wasn't needed.

"I'm so sorry best friend. The crew are outside waiting on an update from you. Everybody is okay. They gone find that nigga."

"Fuck them. They let Bam die and as far as I'm concerned, everybody is dead to me. How is he the only one that got hit? This shit ain't fair and I really don't give a fuck about their concern." You could tell she was offended, but I didn't give a fuck.

"Really bitch? Since we are being brutally honest, Bam is the only one that got hit because his ass was fucking with some niggas he didn't know. Nobody had time to even help him, mother fuckers were trying not to get hit. I'm sorry you are going through this, but this ain't on nobody else. You wrong Pebbles."

"Bitch and you ghost. Get the fuck out of my room before I drag your ass out this bitch. Gone stand your musty ass in my room and talk shit about my nigga, get the fuck on." Throwing up

27

her middle finger, she walked out. Nobody would ever understand because they were still walking around this bitch. Bam was gone, and nobody had his back. I would never forgive them. The doctor finally walked in and I knew I wasn't about to receive good news.

"I'm sorry it took me so long. Unfortunately, the baby did not make it. The bullet did too much damage. You would be lucky to even carry a baby to three months. I'm so sorry, but it was just too much damage." The tears took over and I knew there was no way I would ever be the same.

CHAPTER 4 SHVONNE

A week later they were releasing me from the hospital. I had to do everything from my room and I was a fucking mess. I decided to get Bam cremated. The love of my life was gone, and the shit was tearing me up from the inside. Standing here on the Santa Monica beach, I played music while I spread his ashes over the waters. Stevie Wonder's Never Dream You'd Leave In Summer on my Bluetooth speaker, I thought about all the times we shared.

"I never dreamed you'd leave in summer. I thought you would go then come back home. I thought the cold would leave by summer, but my quiet nights will be spent all alone."

Pouring his ashes, I thought about the first time we made love. I was scared out of my mind. I had just graduated, and the nigga practically drug me to his house. The shit was empty as hell and his mattress was on the floor.

"Damn, all the money you make your ass can't afford a bed? This shit looks like the projects in this bitch."

"Well, you about to get this dirty dick. Quit complaining and come suck this mother fucker. I don't want that pretty shit either."

"Boy, I'm not sucking your dick. You got me fucked up." Not giving a fuck what I said, he grabbed my head and led me down to his lap. Once I got the hang of it, I wasn't scared anymore. After we fucked, he made love to me and left my ass speechless.

"You better let all them niggas know you my girl now. Put your clothes on so we can go to my crib. I'm hungry as hell." Looking at him like he lost his mind, I went off.

"Who house is this? You treating me like I'm some hoe."

"Naw, I had to make sure the pussy was right. If your shit was loose and free, you couldn't be with me. Now be glad you got seran wrap and let's go."

"What the fuck is that?"

"Your pussy fit around my dick like seran wrap. I know you cute, but I can't fuck with no slow bitch." As crazy as it may seem, *that was the happiest day of my life. We been inseparable ever*

since.

"You said then you'd be the life in autumn. Then you said

you'd be the one to see the way. No no no I never dreamed you'd

leave in summer, but now I find my love has gone away. Why

didn't you stay." As Stevie Wonder continued to sing through my

speakers, I cried and spread the last of his remains. All I could do

was laugh at how he came about naming me Pebbles.

"Baby why the fuck is you walking around with your dick

swinging like that? Get dressed so we can go eat. I'm hungry as

hell and you playing."

"As long as we in the house, my ass gone stay naked, so I

can walk up and just bam bam bam in that pussy whenever I feel

like it." This nigga was pumping the air and I couldn't do shit but

laugh. His shit was on soft and it looked funny slapping against his

balls.

"Can you ever be serious damn? You not about to be

fucking me all damn day. My pussy hurt shit. I had to piss leaning on one ass cheek last night. My shit had a heartbeat. You go back

in a bitch gone fuck around and be chaffed."

"I like chaffed pussy too. The bam just gone be a lil slower

and rougher. Pussy gone be sounding like corduroys rubbing

together and I'm not gone give no fucks. Bam Bam Bam." Doing

the pumps again, I couldn't control my laughter. "I gotta keep

fucking you so you can have my baby. That's the only way I can

make sure it's gone stay in there." Shaking my head, I bent over in

the dresser to grab my clothes.

"Can you get dressed?" Walking up behind me, he started

pumping.

"Bam bam bam. Matter fact I'm gone bam your ass so

much I'm gone start calling your ass Pebbles. That's your new

name, Bam Bam and Pebbles. If I hear anybody call you anything

other than Pebbles, I'm gone fuck you for two hours while your

pussy dry. You don't want that kind of punishment." From that day

forward, that's what everybody called me.

Wiping the tears from my eyes, I blew a kiss at the sky and watched the waves. This would be the last time I would see Bam, but he would forever be in my heart. This chapter in my life was over and I had to find a way to push forward. I had to for him.

Grabbing my stuff, I headed off the beach. If I stayed here, I would be here forever. I had memories for days and the shit was only making it worse. Making my way to our house, I stayed strong the best I could. It was hard being in there with his scent all over the house. Bond number nine seemed to be everywhere and I couldn't take it. Walking in my room, I grabbed my luggage and started packing up what I could.

It was almost as if I could hear his laugh. Dropping to the ground, I buried my head in my knees and screamed out a cry. Why was God doing this to me? I didn't deserve to lose everyone and I damn sure didn't deserve to lose Bam. He didn't even allow me to keep my baby and I think that was what was hurting me the most. Feeling someone grab me, I thought I was losing my mind. Looking up expecting to see Bam there, I was disappointed to see

Tiana standing there. I wanted it to be him, I needed it to be Bam.

Breaking down again, she held me until I could no longer cry. The

shit hurt, and I didn't even know how to begin to pick up the

pieces.

"Best friend it's going to be okay. It's going to take a while,

but I promise the shit will start to heal. You just have to stay

strong. What are the bags for?" Looking at her with lost eyes, I

tried to explain what I was feeling.

"I can't stay here anymore. Everyone that I loved, I have

lost in this city. If I stay here I will lose it and he wouldn't want

that for me. Everything reminds me of him, and I can't take it. The

shit might sound selfish but seeing the crew and everyone else

doing well and moving on with life is hard to see. He's gone, but

everyone else is still here." Nodding her head, I didn't know if she

was agreeing with me or processing what I said.

"Bitch I don't want you to go, but I get it. Just promise me

you won't forget about me. Make sure you call me every damn

day. Where are you going? Do you know?"

34

"I'm used to the big city life, so I'm heading to Chicago. When I'm strong enough, I'll come back and visit. I can't say when that will be, but I'll eventually come back. I love you."

"I love you too." Helping me pack, tears fell down my eyes as I sand Stevie Wonder to myself. For some reason, I couldn't stop singing the same part over and over.

"Why didn't you stay?"

CHAPTER 5 SPADE

3 YEARS LATER...

"You telling me that nobody knows why the fuck my shit keeps getting hit? What the fuck am I paying you for if you not there to watch my shit?" This was the second stash house of mine to get hit and pissed was an understatement. My lil nigga GT was in charge of that spot, but his ass had no idea of what the fuck happened.

"Spade I know you pissed, but I can't be in that mother fucker twenty four seven. I got a life just like you do my nigga. I'll find out who did the shit, but you can't put the blame on me." Laughing, I looked over at my best friend Gino. Grabbing my gun, I shot is ass in the head. He had me fucked up. Walking over to his body, I bent down and grabbed my knife. Carving a spade in his jaw, I left my signature on that nigga. That was my thing, and everybody knew it. If you saw a nigga with that spade on his face, his ass crossed me in one way or another and got his ass dealt with.

Jaleel Spade is what my mama named me, but the streets called me Spade. I had the Ace of Spade tatted on my neck when I was fifteen and the shit just stuck. Once I started to take over, I used that shit as my calling card. When I killed a mother fucker, I wasn't ducking. I wanted they ass to know I did it. In Chicago, it's kill or be killed, and I be damned if a nigga like me be six feet under.

"You over here killing niggas in our crew and shit, I heard about some bitches calling they selves trying to take over. That's who you need to be looking for and leave our niggas alone. Who the fuck gone push this shit if these niggas dead? I'm not a bag worker, so know I'm not about to be doing that shit." This nigga Gino been real loose at the lips lately and the shit was starting to piss me off.

"If I want your ass to scrub the floors, that's what the fuck you gone do. All you niggas work for me, make sure you remember that shit. If you want to do something with that big ass

mouth of yours, ask around and find out who the fuck these

bitches are." His jaw flexed, and I looked at him waiting to see if

he was gone do something. When he walked away like I knew he

would, I turned to the rest of the crew.

"Clean this shit up before I Spade you niggas." Heading

into my office, I started counting money. For some reason, the

shit soothed me. The sound from the money machine calmed me.

Gino was starting to rub me the wrong way, but the nigga always

thought he was bigger than what he was. When I met him, he was

a lil nigga trying to take out his boss. Which happened to be my

father. Knowing he was signing his death sentence, I stopped him

from making a dumb ass mistake.

My father never knew what he was up to and we rose up

the ranks together. I've never held that shit over his head, but

now I was starting to wonder if I made a mistake. This nigga was

moving different and if he didn't get right his ass was getting

Spaded. I didn't have time for mother fuckers trying to take me out, and I wasn't blind to bullshit. As if he could hear what I was thinking, he walked in the office. Throwing my money in faster, I needed the sound to calm me quick before shit got ugly.

"Look, everybody knows this is your shit. You make sure of that, but I'm next in command and the shit look flaw as fuck with you reprimanding me in front of the crew. Them lil niggas will start to think they can pull that shit and I ain't with it. Respect me like you want me to respect you." This nigga was dead ass serious, and I had to take a moment, so I didn't spread his shit all over my money.

"I don't give a fuck if you were the only nigga on my team, if you talk to me crazy your ass gone get checked. Now let me know if you feeling like moving something, don't do like you did with my pops. My trigger finger more accurate bitch and it stays ready. You're my best friend and I'm gone need you to act like it. All that flaw shit you been doing lately not gone fly for long. Go find those bitches like I told you." The hate in his eyes was evident and I knew I was gone have to do something about his ass soon.

39

The last thing I needed was to get crossed by a mother fucker I considered my brother, but everything was starting to point that way. I'm trying to give him the benefit of the doubt and not hold his past transgressions against him, but he making this shit hard.

After he left, I decided to head out as well. I needed some air and sitting in this warehouse all day wasn't helping. Jumping in my Cayenne truck, I headed over to my ol girl house. She always knew what to say when I was pissed off. If she cooked, that would make the shit even better. Knocking on the door, I waited for her to answer.

"Why are you beating on my damn door like that. You acting like you did that day them boys chased your ass home. I have never seen a nigga run the sole off his shoes. Your lil ass had one damn sole. Should be calling your ass soleless. Foot loose." She laughed at her own joke and I didn't find shit funny. I wasn't running from the niggas cus I was scared, I was trying to get to my gun. The one day I left that mother fucker at home, a group of niggas tried me.

40

She in here laughing, but those niggas never made it to tell the story. My pops laid their asses out before they hit the porch. I knew my moms had to have been in the street with my pops because her ass didn't blink.

"Mama don't act like you didn't know what it was. I ran those niggas to the place that I wanted them. What you cook? My ass ain't ate all day."

"I'm just saying you looked like a lil girl and I felt so bad for you when they chased your ass home. Your looks never did grow in. You still around here looking like Sheila E. I bet your ass still out here fighting to prove you are a boy. Do you like boys baby?"

"I thought I could come over here and clear my mind, but your ass on that good bullshit today. Fix me a plate real quick, I'll come back and chill."

"Light skinned niggas so sensitive. Your daddy stayed in his feelings. Hell, he looked like he dated boys as well. Mad at me and I ain't seen you bring a girl home since prom." She walked away talking shit, and all I wanted was my plate, so I could get the fuck out of there. Everybody loved my mama because she had no filter, but the shit pissed us off. Everybody that met her fell in love after the first sentence. All you would hear is Ms. Janice is off the chain. I love your mama. Meanwhile, our asses embarrassed than a mother fucker.

Walking back in the front, she slammed the plate against me and causing the damn juice to run out on my Gucci sweater. Shit made me so mad, I almost tripped her bad knee ass.

"See, you be running the fuck out. That's why your old ass over here lonely and shit.

"Nigga please. Your uncle about to be your step daddy. Don't look at me like that, your mama a hoe." Not even responding to her bullshit, I walked out the door.

CHAPTER 6 SHVONNE

"You bitches wasting my time and my time is money. How the fuck we rob an entire trap house and come up with these lil ass scraps? Who idea was it?" Everyone looked at me like I was crazy.

"It was yours nigga." My girl Halle humbled my ass right quick.

"Well why you bitches didn't tell me that shit wasn't the trap house, it was the po house. Broke my nail and shit for four hundred dollars. The house we hit yesterday was a lick, we need more like that shit. No more small jobs."

"My ass only got about a month left in this shit. My pregnant ass getting too big to be out here trying to run and shit. Gino would kill me if he knew what my ass was out here doing." LaLa was the reason for our lick yesterday. That's why I had to have her on my team. It takes a cold hearted bitch to rob your own nigga. The fact that he treated her like shit, made it easier for her to fuck his ass over.

"I think Gino would kill you if he found out you was robbing his ass. I'm sure he don't give two fucks about those other niggas. Especially the shit we did today. That shit was lunch money." It was five of us, so I split the lil ass change up between us. Everyone got their money and left except for me and Halle.

When I moved to Chicago, she was the first person I met. We hit it off right away and became roommates. Even though I had enough money to make it on my own, I knew I was going to need a crew. I didn't know a soul here and she was useful in that way. Norie and Trina were her girls from school, and I found La La. We called ourselves TMC. Take Money Crew and that's what the fuck we did.

Me and Tiana were best friends, but me and these girls were on a different level. We all thought alike and had no problems doing what the fuck we had to do to get that money. It was refreshing to be around them and not think about Bam and

44

the baby all day. For the first year, it was rough on me. Halle

caught me balled up crying a many of nights. She tried her best to

get me to open up, but I wasn't trying to bring my past into what I

had going on today. I needed to stay focused and that's what the

fuck I did.

At first, it was just me and her. We would make a nigga

think we were going to give them some of this pussy, but instead

we robbed their asses blind and went on about our night. One

nigga caught on to what we were about to do, and he fucked

Halle ass up. After that, we decided that shit was too dangerous,

and I ran this idea by her. Word on the street was some nigga

named Spade ran the turfs we were doing our business on, but I

didn't give a fuck.

When he was ready, he could come see me. I would be

waiting on his ass. Bam taught me how to stand my own against

niggas and bitches. My heart didn't pump pussy, it pumped blood

and I was waiting on the day Spade came my way.

For a while, me and Tiana kept in touch. You could tell she really missed me, but I was done with that part of my life. When she kept asking to come out here, I decided to cut that shit off. I couldn't have her fucking up what I had going on.

"Damn bitch. Where your ass just go? I been talking to you for the last five minutes and you ain't heard shit I said."

"My bad girl I was lost in thought. What you say?" You could tell she was irritated she had to repeat herself, but I didn't give a fuck.

"I said do you think using La La while she is this far along is a good idea? She has all the locations, but we putting her in harm's way. My ass would feel bad as fuck if something happened to her or that baby. Do we really need her out here?"

"She knew what she signed up for. If we take her out now, we lose everything. La La is the key to all this shit. Without her, we hitting candy stores and shit. How much danger could she be in? That nigga beat her ass every day. That bitch life is in danger every day. If she doesn't feel sorry for herself, why the fuck am I feeling sorry? Don't start getting soft on me now. As long as she willing to be out here, I'm going to let her." You could tell she didn't agree, but what could she do. La La was brought in by me and I was the only one she answered to.

"If shit goes wrong, just know it's on your ass. Money is not more important than that girl and her baby. Whatever nigga hurt you fucked you up." Before I could think about it, I slapped the next thought out of her ass.

"Don't ever speak on my nigga again. He didn't hurt me, somebody took him away from me. If you want to remain friends, don't ever address me about him."

"I'm gone let you have that because I didn't know, but hit me like that again you gone see who the fuck I am." That shit was funny to me and I laughed in her face, to make sure that she knew it was.

"You heard what the fuck I said. I play a many of games, but that ain't one. My money ain't either, remember that. Just because I don't speak on it, doesn't mean the shit doesn't still hurt me. That's a subject I will never be willing to discuss, and I shouldn't have to. You either trust me to make the best decisions for us or move the fuck around. The shit we do puts us at jeopardy every day. It may be some casualties, but we knew that from jump. We here to get this money ain't no room for a conscience."

"Whatever. I need a ride home. I came with Norie and the bitch left me after getting that lil two dollars." Grabbing my keys to my Benz, we headed out.

"You not out here acting like you need a ride. Bitch about to be out here on that midnight train to Georgia fucking with me. Bring your ugly ass on and throw that shirt away when we get home. Ass out here looking like you got on a Gordon Gatrell."

"Bitch you tried it. This is real silk. Everybody not out there robbing the trap in fur coats and Louie boots."

"What you gone do slide out the window in that smooth ass shirt? Girl bye. Slide your ass in the car."

"Whatever bitch." Heading to our condo, it was always rough for me when I walked in the door. I had to brace myself whenever I got out the car. My dumb ass thought it would be a good idea to make my new condo a replica of the place me and Bam had. That was three years ago, and I think it's time for me to go shopping. This shit was starting to get creepy.

Halle had no idea, she was just happy I offered to pay. When I met her, she was in school busting her ass working at Jimmy Johns. Now she had more money than she ever seen. We were good for each other, but she tried to dig into my past too much.

"Pebbles you good?" My thoughts must be showing through my expression and I needed to get better at that shit.

"Yeah, I'm just tired. I'll holla at you tomorrow." Climbing in my bed, I didn't even remove my clothes. My thoughts had me dreaming of Bam and crying in my sleep. Some days were better than others, but today was a rough one.

CHAPTER 7 GINO

Everybody wanted to try a nigga today, and I was over that shit. Every time Spade slick back ass got in front of the crew, he tried to show off. I was getting tired of him treating me like a lil nigga and he was going to force me to do something about that shit. I've been riding with that nigga since he attempted to save me from his father, but I didn't think I needed saving. His father had no idea I was coming for him, but Spade insisted it was suicide. If I had followed my first mind, all this shit would be mine and his ass would be working for me.

I think the nigga knew I was going to be in charge and he didn't like that shit. His father was getting old and his ass was slipping. I had been robbing his ass blind for a couple of years without him even noticing. For months, I had been planning my takeover and how I was going to kill his ass. To this day, I still don't know how the fuck Spade figured the shit out. No one knew what I was planning, and I covered my tracks carefully.

When he came to me letting me know he knew, I had no choice but to let the shit go. A nigga wasn't trying to lose his life and I knew it would always be another opportunity. At least I thought it was, some niggas from the East Side came and aired his old ass out. They didn't want the territory, all they wanted was his ass dead. The nigga made a lot of enemies and the shit finally caught up with his ass.

King Leel was the nigga everybody wanted to be if you were on the outside looking in. He had all the bitches, the money, and the business sense it took to make it. On the inside, he treated his workers like shit, crossed a lot of people, and didn't give a fuck about nobody but his wife and Spade. I was tired of eating scraps when that nigga was throwing away lobster meals. When they took him out, I thought I would be able to make alliances and take over.

The streets were more scared of Spade young ass than King Leel. His ass offed the niggas that killed his father by his self. Went on their territory and laid they asses out. Knowing that I was trying to take out his father, I was shocked when he asked me to come on the team with him as his right-hand man. To me, that was the perfect opportunity to get what should have been mine. Once Spade actually let me run shit and paid me what I deserved, I thought shit was finally going good for me and I didn't have to take his ass out. Lately, this nigga been moving different and I was sick of the shit.

On top of all the drama I got going on with his ass, my bitch ass baby mama be doing the fucking most. She never does what the fuck I tell her ass to do but wonder why I'm always going upside her fucking head. I've been in this house waiting for her ass an hour, and she hasn't come home yet. If I didn't need her to handle my business, I would have been killed the bitch. It was only one thing I hated more than a disrespectful bitch, and that was a hard-headed hoe. Hearing the garage open, I knew she was about to wobble her big ass in. Before she could even close the door, I soared my shoe at her ass.

"Where the fuck have you been? I told your ass to be in the house and have dinner waiting on me. Why the fuck is the sink full of dishes, but there is no food in this mother fucker? You been out with them bitches all day and now you want to walk your ass in here like shit is good."

"Are you going to let me talk or are you going to keep yelling at me? I been out all day trying to make money for us and you yelling at me like I'm your child. I'm tired and I just want to lay down." See, this is what I meant. Everybody wanted to fucking try me today and I'm not with the shit. Walking over to her fast as hell, I backhanded her like a hoe on the stroll that was twenty dollars short.

"Please Gino don't do this. The baby." Now the bitch wanted to cry about the baby.

"Were you thinking about the baby when you were just talking shit? Shut the fuck up and get your ass in there and cook me some food." Her dramatic ass got up acting like I just put a boot to face on her ass. Not with the theatrics, I went in the front

53

room to wait on my food. If the shit took her to long, I was gone

drag her ass all the way to the basement and make her ass sleep

with the dog.

Not realizing I had nodded off, I looked at the clock and

realized two hours had passed. This bitch must have been up

there making Thanksgiving dinner. She was determined to get her

ass beat the fuck up and I was more than happy to give it to her.

Walking to the kitchen, I was about to beat her ass when I noticed

she was lying on the floor.

"La La if you don't get the fuck up, I promise I'm going to

stomp a mud hole in your ass." When I noticed she didn't move,

my pressure rose up. Looking over at the stove, it pissed me off

more to see the bitch hadn't even started cooking. Grabbing her

by her arm, I drug her to the car and threw her in. "If you lose this

baby bitch you gone lose your life."

I didn't have time for the dumb shit and I damn sure didn't

want to be spending my night hungry in the damn emergency

room because her ass wants to be extra and shit. How the fuck is she in any pain when all I did was slap the hoe. My uncle was a

pimp for years and a bitch ain't died yet from a slap. Acting like

the caring baby father, I carried her inside and explained to the

nurses what was going on with her. After an hour, they finally

called me to the back.

"Sir, has anything happened in the past few hours. It

seems as if she sustained trauma to the head, do you know how it

happened?"

"No I don't. She was supposed to be cooking and after two

hours, I went to check on her. I found her lying on the floor. Is she

going to be okay?"

"She suffered a concussion, but her and the baby will be

fine. Have her to stay on bed rest and take it easy. She must have

fainted, and we don't want her doing that. She could harm herself

or the baby."

"I'll take care of her doc. When can we leave?"

"Tomorrow. I would like to monitor her and make sure she

is okay. I'll leave you two alone, the nurses will bring her something to eat and check her vitals again." I smiled until the

doctor was all the way out of the room. La La was sitting there

with the dumbest look on her face. Grabbing her by her throat, I

got as close as I could.

"Bitch you got me in this fucking hospital because your

soft ass passed out. You better convince these doctors you're

okay, because if you're in here longer than a day they gone have

to keep your ass. Now your ass looking stupid."

"I'm sorry Gino, I don't know what happened."

"Dumb bitches, do dumb shit." The sight of her was pissing

me off. It wasn't always like this, but once she saw I wasn't going

to be the head nigga in charge, she cheated on me with that nigga

Spade. Nobody knew she was my girl at the time, but she knew

that was my nigga. My ass was too sprung and gone off the pussy

to let her go, but I been treating her like shit ever since. There was

no way I could forgive her and I damn sure wasn't about to let her

go and let the next nigga have her.

After that shit, I don't let her anywhere near Spade. If they pass each other in the grocery store, I was gone beat the walk out her ass. When the nigga found out, his ass didn't even apologize. I had to act like she wasn't shit to me and I make sure nobody knows she still my girl. She knew better than to tell somebody or it was gone be over for her ass.

I hated how she had me looking like a fuck nigga, but as long as the bitch did what I wanted, we were good. Nobody knew I was a sucker over the pussy, and I wanted to keep it that way. The nurse walked in with her food and I grabbed the tray acting as if I was prepping it for her. As soon as she left out, I grabbed her shit.

"Gino I'm hungry, I need my food."

"You should have thought about that shit instead of passing the fuck out. I bet your ass cook next time."

CHAPTER 8 SPADE

Riding through the West side of the Chi, I had a lot on my mind. All I could think about were these bitches that might be out here robbing me and the shit I'm going through with Gino. He was starting to become a liability. His demeanor had me second guessing my movements and he keep putting his hands on his baby mama. His ass think I don't know he still with La La, but this chick I fuck with at the emergency room always let me know when they bring they dumb asses in there.

Them mother fuckers be in there at least once a month and that's the kind of heat I don't need. All I wanted to do was make money and be great out here, but these mother fuckers were making it hard to do. Gino had one job, and that was to find these bitches he said was hitting our spot. This nigga was so busy beating bitches, he was slacking in his job. Seeing a group of bitches standing on one of my blocks, I pulled over.

58

I didn't know them, and it was odd seeing them out here when they didn't work for me. If they didn't know who I was, they was about to find out today. Jumping out the car, I adjusted my Prada jogging suit and walked up on them. They looked at me like my ass didn't belong out here and it was my shit. I knew off bat who the ring leader was supposed to be. The bitch was looking at me like she was ready to square up. I don't hit bitches, but I would slap a bitch to sleep.

"Who the fuck are yall and why you standing on my shit like you working?"

"I didn't know your name was city of Chicago. Last I checked, the sidewalks belonged to them. If that's your weak ass rap, you can keep stepping in them old ass last season Prada's. You might wanna hurry up, them bitches look sleepy. They leaning like a mother fucker. You might not make it home." Looking down at my shoes, I knew the bitch had to be lying. I just spent seven hundred on these bitches, so I know my shit was tight. If she wasn't fine as fuck, I would have slapped her ass.

Looking her over, I was trying to clap back but her shit was on point. High yellow wasn't normally my type, but shorty was on point. Her hair was down her back and you could tell it wasn't weave. Baby girl was slim, but she wore that shit well. She had on some Louie boots and some jeans that hugged all her curves. Her short shirt let me see it wasn't a belly in sight. My dick was getting hard, and that wasn't good since I had on jogging pants. I didn't need the bitch clowning me like I didn't get pussy.

"Don't play with me, I'm sure you know who the fuck I am. If you don't, you about to find out quick. Keep playing with me and your lil ass gone get tossed up out here. Now, why the fuck you on my shit?" Her sexy ass rolled her eyes and my dick jumped.

"Because I wanna be. The fuck." Her friends laughed, and I was tired of playing games with lil mama. Walking up as close as I could, our lips damn near touched. The perfume she was wearing had me wanting to slide my tongue in her mouth. Trying to get back on track, I grabbed her by the neck. I was about to threaten her ass when she slapped piss from my dick hole. My reflex reaction was to grab my gun. When I pointed it at her, she didn't

even flinch. You could tell she was used to this shit and that made

me intrigued. I wanted to know shorty's story, but I knew she was

going to make the shit hard to do. Trying not to let her know that I

wanted her, I kept my game face on.

"You bitches got ten seconds to get the fuck off my block

before yall asses get Spaded. Not breaking my stare, you could tell

the girls with her was scared.

"Pebbles come on before you get our ass killed. I got a son,

I'm not trying to die today." She didn't look like a Pebbles, but it

was a cute name for her. The mother fucker had the nerve to

push me and storm off. They jumped in their separate cars and I

jogged over to my truck. I wasn't letting her get away that easy.

Keeping my distance, I followed her to a condo complex. I'm glad

her shit was facing the street and I could see which one was her's.

My ass wasn't out here trying to look like Marvin off Player's Club.

She though the shit was over, but it wasn't. Her lil ass was

gone pay for slapping me. This dick was gone tame her smart a whether she knew it or not. Pulling off, I knew I wasn't gone be

able to fuck her ass, so I drove to this chick house I been fucking

with. Me and Jontanae been fucking for a few months now. She

had some good ass pussy, but I could never make her my bitch.

She had a football team of kids and them mother fuckers was bad

as hell. Parking my truck, I used my key to walk in. Her ass knew

better than to fuck another nigga, so I never had to announce

myself. Even though she wasn't my girl, I don't play that

community pussy.

"J, where you at?" Like always, she came running to me

ready to do anything I asked of her.

"Hey baby, I cooked. You want a plate?"

"Fuck no. You know damn well your ass can't cook.

Besides, I'm trying to feed you." Blushing, she looked over her

shoulder and walked over to the couch. "Are your kids sleep? I'm

not trying to be out here digging in your guts and your kids bring

 my bad ass out here watching."

"They know not to come out when I got company."
Grabbing my dick out of my pants, she immediately put my dick in
her mouth. This why she could never be my bitch. Her ass didn't
care if her kids saw us or not. The suction thing she did with her
mouth brought me back. My dick was standing at attention and I
had to kick my shoes off and get comfortable.

"Fuck girl. You must have missed a nigga." Her only
response was guzzling down my dick. My shit was hitting her
throat and I was ready to bust, but I needed some pussy. Pebbles
was on my mind and I had some aggression to get out. Pushing
her off me, I grabbed a condom out of my pocket and slid the shit
on.

Pushing her over the couch, I slid my dick up and down her
slit and pushed it in. For her to have so many kids, her pussy was
tight. I loved when pussy gripped my dick. A nigga didn't like that
slip and slide. My dick big as hell, so if a pussy can make my shit
seem small I ain't with that shit.

"Fuck Spade. This your pussy baby." This bitch was screaming like her kids wasn't in the next room. The shit was a turn off and I needed to hurry up and bust this nut. My intentions were to leave after I fucked, but she did a trick that almost made me fall asleep in the pussy. She was throwing that baby factory all over this dick. Before I knew it, I was filling my condom up. When I pulled out, I could barely make it to the bathroom and flush the condom. Washing myself off, I went back and sat on the couch. I needed to catch my breath but fell asleep.

My ass didn't wake up for five hours. Looking around, I couldn't find my shoes. One of her bad ass kids done jacked me for my shit. Not even wanting to be bothered with they lying, thieving ass, I left them bitches and took my ass home. She gone have to do something about them kids if she wanted to keep getting this dick. Them damn kids don't have no manners.

CHAPTER 9 SHVONNE

Driving off from Spade, I was pissed the fuck off. Not only did he try and treat me like I was weak ass bitch, but the nigga was fine as hell. It took everything in me to stay pissed but his ass was making it hard. Spade had to be about 6'2, long ass dreads but he wore them curly, and golds on his bottom teeth. His yellow complexion made his tats show and them bitches were everywhere. I wasn't used to this kind of nigga. Back home, they didn't look like this and it was hard for me to keep a straight face.

When he walked up on me, I paid attention to the tat of a Spade on his neck. It was unique and I'm sure no one else in the world had that mother fucker. As he threw out useless threats, I stared intently at that tat. Coming back to reality, I slapped the shit out of his ass. Halle told the nigga my name and I was pissed. As soon as we got in the house, I lit into her ass.

"Don't ever in your fucking life do that shit again. Have you lost your damn mind?" She had the nerve to look like she didn't know what I was talking about. One thing I hated was a slow

bitch.

"What are you talking about Pebbles? Your ass always got

a fucking attitude. Damn. Loosen the fuck up already. If you not

going the fuck off, your ass is somewhere in a corner crying. Get a

fucking grip." You would have thought I ran track as fast as I went

across the room and jumped over the couch. The bitch wasn't

even smart enough to duck even though she saw me coming.

Punching the bitch in her mouth, I prayed her ass swung back. Of

course, the punk bitch sat there looking shocked.

"Let me explain something to you. Everything you know

about me, it's because I told you. Don't act like you fucking know

me. We cool but bitch I will beat the fuck out of your ass. I

promise I'm the one you don't want as an enemy and if you ever

come at me like that again, you will have one. Play pussy and get

fucked."

"Wow. You really hit me Pebbles? I thought we were

better than that. It's cool."

66

"When a bitch says it's cool, I take that as a threat. Let me know if you feel like leaping, I stay ready. The next time a nigga come up on us acting like he wants beef and you say my name, you won't make it back. That's not a threat, it's a promise." Walking out the door, I needed to clear my head. This bitch pissed me off, but I didn't want us to be into it. Our living arrangement worked, and she was the closest person I had here.

Realizing I left my keys in the house, I decided to walk. It wasn't that cold out and the breeze helped me clear my mind. There was so much flowing through my shit, I didn't realize I had been out here for hours. The breeze was therapeutic, and it helped me to calm down. Standing up, I decided to head home since it had gotten chilly out.

Halfway down the block, a truck drove behind me as if it was following me. A bitch was so pissed off, I walked outside without my gun. Now I was kicking my own ass for being a hot head and not thinking. Even though I wasn't a punk, a bitch had to be smart. It was time to put knees to elbows. I wasn't trying to end up on the ID channel. Without looking back, I took the fuck

off. You could hear the car speed up and for the first time in my

life, a bitch was scared.

What the fuck would they want with me? My ass is small,

my head mediocre, and my pussy be dry sometimes. Halle would

have a field day with this shit, she would probably want me at the

bottom of the Mississippi River. Reflex wanted me to turn around,

but experience told my ass bitch keep going. Feeling some strong

arms wrap around me, I knew it was over for me.

"Why the fuck your scary ass running? You was all tough

earlier slapping niggas and shit. Now you done turned into a

whole hoe. I was just trying to give you my jacket damn." Realizing

it was Spade, my fear immediately went away. Turning around, I

was ready to beat his ass for scaring me like that.

"Why the fuck would I want that old ass Jacket? I don't

rock nothing but the new shit. I'm good."

"Your mean ass don't ever calm the fuck down, but I know

something that will. Keep on, you gone get this dick in your life.

I'm trying to be nice, but if your ass keep pushing me you gone see why the streets fear me."

"Blah Blah Blah you always talking about what you gone do and who scared of your ass. You're twenty pounds from being on a save the world commercial. Eighteen cents a day ass nigga." I tried to control my breathing when he walked up on me. The nigga was sexy as fuck, but I wasn't ready to take it there. This nigga grabbed me by my neck and forced his tongue in my mouth. I was about to get into the kiss until the wind blew and a smell hit me. Breaking the kiss, I slapped the shit out of him again for the second time today.

"Nigga I know you not over here kissing me and you just came from fucking a bitch. If you ate that hoe pussy and kissed me, I will kill your hoe ass." Spade actually smirked, and we were about to go the fuck at it.

"You wouldn't give me none. A nigga has needs." When he saw the fire in my eyes, he started laughing. "I did fuck a bitch, but I don't eat pussy like that. You good." Relaxing, I still couldn't believe he fucked a bitch and all up in my face. Not knowing what to say, I looked down at the ground. Realizing he had on some different shoes, I started laughing.

"I see you took off those last season Pradas. Let me find out I hurt your lil ego."

"Naw the bitch I was fucking got some bad ass kids. One of them stole my shit." We both laughed, and I couldn't figure out if he was telling the truth or talking shit. He didn't look like the type that had to lie, so knowing it actually happened caused me to laugh harder.

"This lil back and forth was nice, but it's cold out here and I'm ready to go lay it down. It's been a long ass day and some rude ass nigga pulled a gun on me today. I'm just ready to lay it down and start the fuck over."

"You didn't want to answer my question, and I don't play that shit. The streets are mine, and if I don't know who out here working on my shit, I'm questioning they ass. Get in, I'll take you home."

"I don't want you to know where I stay. You pulled a gun on me once, it won't be a next time."

"Shorty I already know where you stay. I told you these are my streets. Now get in, I'm not going to tell you again." Turning around, I started walking down the street. That nigga don't run me, and I wasn't about to let him think he could start. At least that's what I thought until he snatched me up and threw me in the truck. "Look, we are not about to go through this every time we see each other. I don't like disrespectful, smart mouth women."

"Nigga drive before I change my fucking mind. I done gave in and let your pressed ass take me home, so do it. Shut the fuck up damn. Matter fact, why do you always feel the need to let someone know what you will do to them?"

"Because I will, plain and simple. I don't give second chances, and I don't allow mother fuckers to get at me first. Me telling you to shut the fuck up is a warning, anything after that is a bullet." Him saying that made me feel some type of way.

71

"So, you kill people just because? I know I'm a hot head, but I have to have a reason to kill someone. That shit ain't cool."

"I didn't say it was cool, but it's me. I watched my father get gunned down because he didn't think a nigga would pull the trigger. Have you ever had to watch someone you loved with all of you die in front of you? That shit does something to a person." I wanted to scream YES, I KNOW. I RELIVE THE SHIT EVERYDAY. Fighting back tears, I responded.

"No, I haven't. It must have been hard for you. I'm sorry you went through that." The rest of the way it was quiet. It's like neither of us knew what to say. When he pulled up to my house, he reached for a hug, but I pulled away and ran in the house. Tonight, I cried myself to sleep thinking about Bam.

CHAPTER 10 LA LA

Baby you don't pay me no mind. You act like you don't love me no more.

Maybe you need space or some time. Your attitude is unpredictable.

I don't want to make you unhappy if you not happy then you're free to go on.

Cus I don't want you staying around if I make you so miserable.

If you don't want me then don't talk to me. Go ahead and free yourself.

My miserable ass been in this house feeling sorry for myself singing Fantasia Free Yourself and I didn't know how to get out of my funk. This shit with Gino was driving me crazy and I didn't know what else to do. He was punishing me for the one mistake I made, but the nigga cheated on me with every bitch around the way. Every time I looked up, I was fighting a bitch over my nigga. Make that shit make sense. They were acting as if I was in the wrong for fucking they man. Bitches was a trip that way. I wanted to tell they ass, bitch you can have him. Bet fifty dollars to a bucket of shit they give his ass back.

After all the lies, cheating, and disrespect, the nigga had the nerve to be beating my ass left and right. I tried my best to do everything he asked to right my wrongs, but none of that matters. It's something he refuses to let go of and I don't know if I can take much more. Every time he hit me, my baby was at risk. The hospital knew what was going on, but they couldn't do shit about it because I lied for him every time we went.

My life has gone to shit, and my parents are so ashamed of what I have become, they don't even mess with me. The streets talk, and they know exactly what Gino ass was doing to me. It wasn't always like this. In the beginning you couldn't have told me he wasn't my soul mate. The nigga had so much swag. A brown skinned Son of a God. He was outside with his shirt off, and tats were everywhere. He was a member of the beard gang and it was long and groomed. You could see the print in his basketball shorts and I just had to have him. A bitch walked over to him and shot my shot. His ass turned me down like a collar on a crisp dress shirt.

Walked off with three bitches on his arm. That should have been my sign that I wanted no parts of what he was offering, but hook line and sinker I was gone. Women aren't prepared to get turned down by a nigga, our egos can't take it. If a nigga ever wants a chick, all he has to do is act like he doesn't want her. I chased behind him so long, my asthma kicked in on a couple of occasions. The last time I saw him at the basketball courts playing ball and my ass was cheering the loudest. That nigga turned and winked at me, and that was all it took. After the game he knew my ass was coming over. I've been wrapped up in his spell since.

It felt good as hell to be on his arm. Everywhere we went, he bragged on how he had the baddest bitch in the game. My goofy ass would smile from ear to ear. When he introduced me to Spade, I almost passed the fuck out. It was in that moment, that I realized I may have chased the wrong damn friend. Bitches need to see all the friends and family first before they start choosing. Been done chose wrong and can't do shit about it but stare. The funny thing is, I was looking at him all goofy and shit, but his ass never glanced up at me. Spade was texting and gave my ass a head nod. Walked off and jumped in his car. I could have looked like a crack head on the first of the month, and he wouldn't have noticed.

When I got tired of Gino cheating on me and the different bitches trying to fight me, I went out one night to Arnie's the strip club and got drunk as hell. On my way out, I bumped right into Spade. This time he noticed me, but he didn't say a word. That nigga grabbed me and pulled me to his car. My ass was nervous thinking he was driving me to Gino, but we ended up at his house. We never made it past the front room and I tried to give him the best sex of his life.

After we were done, his phone rung he told someone they could come in he was home and told me to get the fuck out.

Embarrassed wasn't the word, I felt like shit as I got dressed. My life flashed before my eyes as I pulled my panties up and came eye to eye with Gino. He never reacted, and I walked out the door. Standing at his truck, I waited for him to come out. When he did his ass told me to walk home and I better walk.

A bitch didn't make it home to damn near the next morning. When I got there, he beat my ass for hours. When he got tired, he took a break and started back up when he got his next breath. This has been my life ever since. Often times, I blamed myself for being stupid enough to sleep with Spade. What I didn't understand was how he couldn't forgive me, but I forgave him a many of days.

I sat in the house depressed and bruised up until I met Pebbles. She invited me to join her crew, and I happily accepted. They were my family and that was the only time I felt like I belonged and needed. They knew whenever I was getting my ass beat cus I wouldn't come around until my bruises healed. Hearing the door slam, I knew he had an attitude. When I had this baby, my ass was getting the fuck out of dodge. I've been saving money

and I was going to walk away from all this shit.

"Why the fuck you in here listening to this sad ass music.

Turn this shit off. I don't wanna hear that dumb ass music."

Grabbing the remote, I turned it off. I knew when he was trying to

bait me. Getting up, I walked to the kitchen and grabbed his plate.

Warming it up, I grabbed a soda and took it over to him. Before I

could walk off and leave him to eat, the nigga threw the plate at

me. The food was falling down from my hair, and I couldn't stop

the tears.

"What happened out there today? You come in here being

mean to me for no reason. I'm trying baby, but if you don't want

me to, I can leave."

"Me and your side nigga keep getting into it and if you

think I'm gone let you leave so you can go be with that nigga, you

got me fucked up. I hit your dumb ass with the plate because the

shit was still cold. Pay attention and you won't get hit. Now fix me

another plate and get the fuck out. If you pass out again, I'm gone

78

stomp your ass and this time you not going to the hospital."

Crying, I went in the kitchen and did what he asked me to do. This time, I let it warm up two minutes longer to make sure it was all the way warm. Walking the plate back to him, he put it in his mouth and burned his tongue.

"You got me fucked up. Bitch you trying to be funny, but we gone see who get the last laugh." Standing up, I knew he was about to fight me. All I could do was close my eyes and pray for better days.

CHAPTER 11 SPADE

Even though Pebbles tried to continue to act tough last night, I knew she wanted me. Her eyes told a different story and I didn't mind working to get a chick like her. All the bitches I knew threw themselves at me and a nigga like me didn't like easy pussy. Even Jontanae didn't throw the pussy at me, she just let a nigga do what the fuck he wanted once I dicked her down.

Looking at Pebbles, she seemed to be strong as hell. Not scared of nothing and has it all together. Her strong demeanor will have you thinking her ass don't care about shit, but her eyes told a different story. Even though she said no, I could tell she lost somebody close to her. I wanted to hug her, but I knew she wouldn't let me. Her eyes were sad as fuck and it made a nigga like me weak as hell to see that shit.

Whoever hurt her, or she loved and lost broke her down bad. I was going to be the one to heal her though. I needed an angle to get in, but once I did, I was gone break them walls down little by little. That tough girl shit was an act, but I was happy as

fuck she wasn't a push over. Weak women make my nuts itch.

They need to get a fucking back bone, because a nigga like me will

run all over they ass.

"Did you hear me nigga?" Looking up, I saw Gino standing

there looking at me like I was crazy. His ass came in quiet as hell

and shit like that made me look at him funny.

"Naw what's up? You found out anything for me?" The

attitude in his voice was evident.

"It was definitely a group of bitches. A crackhead said they

saw five chicks leaving out of the trap. I don't know who they are,

but now we know where to start." Looking at him like he was

crazy, I stood up.

"You telling me this like you done found out some new

shit. The last time I saw you, I knew the same thing then, that I

know now. I'm still no closer to my money. Do I need to make

somebody else my right hand? You moving funny, but I got

something that will make you move right my nigga." His jaw line

jumped, and I laughed.

"I'm the one out here doing the footwork. All your ass do

is sit in this fucking warehouse and talk shit. I don't see you out

here trying to find out who the fuck these bitches are. Miss me

with the bullshit." I swung at the nigga like I was trying to

rearrange his jaw and it connected fast and hard. Tired of his

mouth, I gave him a few more. Gino jumped up ready to fight, but

the look in his eyes told me he knew that shit wouldn't be a smart

move.

"On King Leel I dare your ass to come at me strong again.

You pushing me my nigga and you know how that shit gone play

out. The envy and jealousy all over your face, and that shit not a

good look. Get your shit together or lose your life." The nigga

walked off and punched hole in the wall. I knew he wanted to

fight, but he wasn't ready to go to war with me. Laughing, I sat

back at my desk when the shit hit me. Five girls. Pebbles was out

there with three other bitches the day I saw her. Why were they on my block? They had to be the girls that were robbing me.

Grabbing my keys, I jogged out to my truck and headed to her

house. This girl had to have a death wish or something. No one in

their right mind would rob me if they knew who I was. Nobody

but Pebbles tough ass.

Pulling over, I walked to her condo and beat the hinges off

her door. Finally, someone answered. It wasn't Pebbles, but it was

one of the girls that she was with that day. You could see the

crazy look on her face trying to figure out why I was there.

"Where Pebbles at?" They were like night and day. You

could see the fear in her eyes and it was written on her face.

Pebbles would have slapped me for showing up at her door.

"Umm I don't know. If you step on the porch, I can see if

she is here." This bitch thought I was dumb.

"I'm straight, I'll wait right here." Walking off, you can see

her ass trembling. Lil ass booty cheeks were even shaking like they

were scared. I waited until she went inside of one of the

bedrooms and I followed behind her. Pebbles was definitely here,

83

she just wasn't sure on if she should let me in. I was about to

make it easy on both of them. No matter what they thought, I was

bringing my ass in. Busting in the door, you could tell Pebbles was

cursing the girl out.

"Can you excuse us. We need to talk." The girl looked at

Pebbles for approval and I laughed at how shook she had her.

After she left the room, I was next for the tongue lashing.

"Why the fuck are you just showing up at my house.

You're not a bad looking guy, you can't be this fucking desperate.

If you can't get one bitch to show you some attention, maybe you

need to work on your weak ass game." Pulling my gun from my

waist, she instantly stopped talking.

"Did you and your bitch ass friends rob me?" Even though

she didn't say anything, the look in her eyes told it all. "I'm not

going to ask you again." The scared look stayed all of ten seconds

and then her hard demeanor returned.

"Yeah and? We didn't know who you were and that's what

we do. You standing in the presence of the Take Money Crew. If you don't want your shit took, then put it the fuck up. You acting

like the money we got gone break your ass." Her ass was on the

verge of dying, but here she was talking shit like I wasn't holding a

gun on her.

"Do you realize that your life is in danger right now?"

"If you gone do it then go ahead. I wasn't supposed to be

here anyway." When she bit her lip, you could see she was

fighting away tears. I noticed her hair was no longer straight, but

it was in curls and she looked innocent as hell. Without thinking, I

rubbed my finger down her face and the tears fell without her

wanting to. I don't know what her story was, but right now I just

wanted to make her tears go away.

Grabbing her, I kissed her with more passion than I knew I

had inside of me. I was shocked when she started kissing me back.

Not wanting to give her time to think, I pushed her gown up and

lifted her around my waist. Sliding my jogging pants down, I slid

her down on my dick. When she let out a scream, it made my shit

go on brick. Her pussy was so tight, either she was a virgin, or it's

85

been a while since she had sex. The shit was so tight, I couldn't

move. I had to give myself a minute before I came quick. Pebbles

was the type to clown a nigga and I couldn't have that shit.

"Move up and down slow. You need to get used to my

size." She tried to do what I was asking, but it was hard for her.

Grabbing her ass, I decided to take over. It will hurt her, but I may

as well get it over with. Slamming one hard time, she screamed

out and I felt bad for her. Not bad enough to ease up though.

Once I got all the way in, I knew I would never want to be out of

this pussy.

Once I started bouncing her up and down on my shit, she

finally caught the hang of it and started throwing that shit back.

She was going so hard, I damn near lost my balance. Walking over

to the bed, I laid her down and took my clothes off.

"Turn over." For the first time since I met her, she did what

I asked. Climbing behind her, I admired the sight in front of me

and dug in.

"Damn nigga slow down. The pussy not going nowhere. Thirsty ass acting like he ain't got no pussy before." Tired of her smart ass mouth, I was about to teach her ass a lesson.

"You gone learn to shut the fuck up today." Gripping her as hard as I could, I started beating that pussy up. I was pushing my shit in her long and hard. She couldn't keep up.

"Please slow down. Oh my Gawwddd. I can't take it." Slapping her on the ass, I kept beating that shit up.

"Naw you were just talking big shit. Talk it now with your tough ass." Slapping her ass again, her pussy got soaked and her body started shaking. "Cum on this dick." Her body started shaking, I pulled out and sucked that pussy from the back. That shit was so sweet it was almost better than being inside of her.

"Fuck Spade, I'm cumming again." Continuing to suck on her clit, I waited on her juices to coat my tongue. When her body started shaking again, it was time for me to get my nut. Sliding back inside, I slowed down. Looking at my dick sliding in and out of her shit had me ready. My dick started jumping and I pulled out and shot it on her ass. I was gone off her ass, but I wasn't ready for no kids. I knew she had me because this was the first girl I went inside without a condom.

"Can you close the door all the way when you leave, Halle ass gone do the most. I know she heard my ass." Pebbles was like a nigga. She just fucked me and put me the fuck out.

"Yeah, I got you." I would just have to shower when I got home. Throwing my clothes and shoes on, I left out and shut her door. Once I got in my truck, I couldn't stop smiling. I knew I would eventually tear her walls down, and today started that process. Was I pissed that her and the Dreamettes robbed me? Yes.

At the end of the day, they had their hustle and I had mine. That shit was out the window now that we were fucking around, but I was gone let that shit go off the strength of Pebbles and me wanting her. It's not like they even put a dent in my pocket. They ass stole lunch money. If she thought she could get away with it again, then I would have to make an example out of her ass. I would hate to kill her because I really wanted her ass, but I couldn't let that shit fly twice. Especially since she knows a nigga now. That would be outright disrespect.

My ass was so deep into thought about her ass, I didn't see the car behind me until it was too late. Shots rang out and I had to take cover. Even though I had my gun, I couldn't even try to shoot back. The bullets were coming in fast and I was just trying to stay alive. When the gun fire stopped, I grabbed my gun and looked around. It was nothing and nobody there. Just me and a bunch of shell casings. If this nigga Gino shot at me, tonight was his last night on earth. I've never had a nigga shoot at me because I never gave them the chance. Driving to the warehouse for an emergency meeting, I was pissed.

CHAPTER 12 SHVONNE

I couldn't believe me, and Spade had sex. The shit was so good a bitch had to rethink her life. He had my ass trembling and I ain't never had that done before. Don't get me wrong, Bam was good as hell in bed, but it was nothing like this. I've never been with anyone else, but Spade had to have the best dick in the world. He got that nigga we fucked so we go together kind of dick. Whoever the bitch he was fucking before me was gone need to move the fuck around. My ass was on a mission and Spade was about to be sprung.

It was time for me to start watching videos and tutorials. My sex and head was gone have to be on point. I put his ass out because if we had cuddled and laid the fuck up, a bitch was gone be begging him to move in and I would be putting Halle the fuck out. Knowing I needed to keep some kind of sanity, I made him leave. After he was gone, me and Halle made a run and I've been in the house since. TMC haven't robbed anybody since Spade put

90

us off the corner so all of our ass was bored. Knowing we needed

some type of girl's night, I wanted to see if they were down.

"Halle, let's go out tonight. I'm sick of being in this house

crying and I'm in a good mood. I'm ready to turn the fuck up. You

down?" Her goofy ass started smiling and shit.

"Let me find out Spade fucked your ass into a good as

mood and shit. If that's all it took for your mean ass to smile and

loosen up, I would have been told him where we lived. I'm down

like a mother fucker. I'll call Norie and Trina. You hit up La and see

if she down. I'm so excited." Her ass was in my face jumping

around and shit. I guess good dick do make you happy and shit. If

she had done this shit a week ago, I would have been ready to

slap her ass.

"You so extra. Quit being silly and call them so they can

start getting ready. I don't do people, so I need to get a table. It's

been a long time since I been out, and I need tonight to be lit."

"I got you bitch." Halle walked off, and I thought about La

La. No one has heard from her ass and that only meant one thing,

Gino had beat her ass. I wish a nigga would try to put his hands on me, them bitches would be cut the fuck off. Dialing her number, I called her and hoped she would answer.

"Hey Pebbles, what's going on?" She sounded tired as hell and not sleepy. Like she was tired of life.

"We haven't heard from you? What's going on? You good?"

"Yea this baby kicking my ass." Rolling my eyes, I wanted to say naw, that nigga kicking your ass. Knowing it wasn't gone change anything, I left it alone.

"Anyway girl, what you got going on today?"

"Nothing, reading these books that just came out. Mind on Goddess Feelings on Savage by B Moni and Khiaere and Phy by Mel Dau. Shit been having me all in my feelings."

"Girl I don't give a fuck about no books. Your ass always doing that shit. Do it look like I'm trying to read about somebody else happy ass life and I'm out here robbing niggas and shit just to make it?" Every time Gino beat her ass, this is the shit she does.

92

Listen to sad ass music and read books about another mother

fucker being happy. Last time it was some girl named AJ Davidson

that had her in her feelings. Talking about Dope Boys Need Love

Too. Naw bitch, you need love. You the one in the house

miserable as hell.

"You should try it sometimes. The shit therapeutic, it calms

me." Being away from a nigga and living your life without getting

beat would calm you too. That's what I wanted to say, but I was in

a good mood.

"Me and the girls are going out tonight and we wanted

you to go with us. We all need some fresh air and it would help

you. Please, you know how long it's been since I been out." You

could hear her take a deep breath.

"Okay." Now my ass was smiling doing a dance. Hanging

up, I went in my closet to look for something to wear when my

phone rung. I thought it was La La calling me back to cancel, but it

was Tiana. Hesitating, I answered.

"Bitch what's up. Your ass don't know me no more huh? Why the fuck I never hear from you? I miss your raggedy ass." Laughing, it felt good to hear her voice.

"Hey best friend. My ass getting ready to go to the club. I need a turn up. All I do is work."

"How is taking niggas money work? Besides, you need to put me on. Let me come down there and live with you. I ain't got shit going on here and I miss you." I've always tried to keep Tiana away from this life. She was hood as hell, but not a criminal.

"I'll let you know best friend. We will talk about this later. I don't want to be late. Make sure you call me tomorrow or something." You could tell she was disappointed from the silence.

"Okay. Have fun." Hanging up, I tried to hurry and think of something else. It wasn't just her lack of streets that had me rushing off the phone. Tiana was my past and made me think about Bam too much. I was in a good mood and wanted to keep it that way.

Settling on a black Chanel fitted mini dress, I grabbed my red Chanel heels and clutch to match. It was time to get ready.

****

Norie and Trina rode together, while me and Halle went to pick up La La. Her pregnant ass came out the house in a sexy ass dress with her hair pent up in a ball. She looked cute as hell to be almost nine months pregnant. You could tell her ass was sneaking the way she kept looking around. Me and Halle couldn't do shit but laugh at her ass. Watching her try to climb in the car fast with that big ass belly was a sight to see.

"Hurry up and pull off. Gino is gone out, but I don't know if he left something and gone come back. I'm down to go anywhere but the Blue Note. That's where he going tonight." Shaking our head as we continued to laugh had her pissed off.

"We definitely not going to no damn Blue Note. Ain't that where the old people go drink and shit?"

"Naw, they done turned the shit into a club. Shit be cracking in there now. Where we going then?" You could tell she was still worried.

"To the Skybox. Far away from his ass. Now relax. You looking too cute to be worried about a nigga that's out and not thinking about your ass. Now chill the fuck out before you blow my night." Seeing her relax a little was a good thing, and I headed to the club.

When we pulled up, you could tell it was about to be lit inside. The line was around the corner. Norie and Trina was waiting on us and we all headed to the front.

"Yall know I don't do lines, so I'm about to work my magic. I'll take one for the team, so we can get in." Norie ass didn't mind fucking a nigga for perks. She was a good bitch to have on the team. Approaching the bouncer, he was fine as hell.

"Fuck that, we can tag team his ass." Trina was ready to fuck the nigga as well. I laughed as her and Norie high fived. We stood back and let Norie flirt with him and watched them

LOCKED DOWN BY HOOD LOVE   LATOYA NICOLE

exchange numbers. Two minutes later, we were walking in. The bitch did what she said, and she was alright with me. It's always good to have a hoe on your team as long as she not trying to fuck your man.

The inside was packed as well, but I knew I wanted a table. Standing at the bar waiting to pay for one, I spotted Spade and some guys in VIP. When I saw a girl sit on his lap, I didn't think about shit else. That was not a part of the plan. His ass needed to think about me and only me. The girls were looking at me as they followed me power walking to Spade's section. They had no idea what I was on, but they were about to find out. Security tried to stop me, but he was too slow. My ass jumped that rope like I was playing double dutch.

Before anybody could see what was happening, I grabbed a bottle off the table and hit the girl in the head with it. Bitch couldn't even take a hit. After she fell to the floor, I refused to let her make it. I tried to stomp the bitch edges together. Spade jumped up and grabbed me. You could tell he was amused, but I didn't see shit funny. This nigga thought I was a game, but he was about to see how I got down.

"Pebbles baby calm down. It's not that fucking serious." When he saw I was good, he let me go. Reaching down to grab the girl, he tried to help her out. That shit pissed me off more.

"Oh, you checking on bitches now? That's what we do, we see if bitches are good now. Let me give you something to check nigga." At this point, I didn't give a fuck who my punches hit. Him or her ass, but I started throwing haymakers. His crew was laughing hard as hell, while he concentrated on not getting hit.

"Jontanae just go home. I'll call you later." You could tell she wasn't pleased about that, but I was pissed he said he would call her. Slapping the liquor out his pores, I jumped in his face.

"Who you gone call? The only number your ass better dial is 911 after I fuck you up." Grabbing me around my arms so I couldn't hit him again, he whispered so only I could hear him.

"You got ten seconds to calm down or I'm gone murder that pussy tonight. No mercy. You won't be able to sit down for a week." Knowing how he had my shit throbbing the last time, I got

my shit together and tried to sit down. Snatching me, he pulled

me on top of him and just like that, I was happy again.

"Where the fuck you find this crazy ass girl? She sent this

mother fucker up." Some guy with Spade was laughing hard as

fuck. My girls finally relaxed and sat down with them.

"She robbed me the other day." Everybody including the

girls had a shocked look on their faces. I never told them he knew.

"Oh, she must got that witch craft pussy. I don't want that

kind of pussy. Fuck that. Hey, but some of that money was mine.

I'm gone need my cut back." Everybody started laughing, and I

turned to Spade.

"You're mine. Don't let me have to tell you that shit

again." He laughed like he thought I was joking. When he kissed

me, I was ready to leave that bitch. We all started dancing and

having a good time until we heard a slap over the music. Looking

up, La La was holding her face and Gino was standing there

looking like the devil himself.

"You got me fucked up. Bring your dumb ass on. Lying ass told me you were staying at home reading, but you all in this nigga face." I wondered what nigga he was talking about.

"Gino, I begged her to come. She was in the house reading. Come in and have a good time with us. We celebrating me locking Spade down. Dick got handcuffs on it." Everybody laughed but Gino and Spade. His jaw line was moving fast as fuck, but he didn't say a word. I guess he didn't want to look like a weak nigga, so Gino came and sat down. The fear I saw in La La's eyes pissed me off. Turning towards Spade, I could see he was in another world as well.

Trying to lighten his mood, I started grinding on him. I twerked on his dick like I was on the dance floor. When his dick got hard, I knew he was no longer mad.

"Keep on, you gone get fucked tonight."

"That's what I want." For the first time since Gino walked in, he smiled.

CHAPTER 13 GINO

Shit was getting out of hand, but I was about to get this shit in order. First Spade thought he was going to get away with putting his hands on me. That nigga hit me like I was a bitch that owed him money. I wanted so bad to lay that lil nigga out, but in due time. It's a time and place for everything and if I had hit him in the warehouse, I wouldn't be here to tell the story. That nigga supposed to be my best friend and he was treating me like some lil nigga off the street.

Leaving out, all I could do was punch the wall. That's how pissed I was, but at that time, it was all I could do. When I got home, this bitch La La was trying me. After laying hands on her, shit was going good.

Me and La La chilled out all today, and as crazy as it seemed, we actually had a good day. Shit was smooth, and she didn't do anything to piss me off. I had to leave out to handle some business, and when I came back home she had dinner done

101

right. A nigga was ready to tear into her guts, but Spade called my

phone.

"Be at the warehouse in twenty minutes. If you're late, pay

the consequences." Before I could respond, his bitch ass hung up.

Looking over at La La, she actually looked like she was sad I was

leaving.

"Be naked when I get back. Daddy gone fuck you like I

used to. I want you to do that thing I like. You got me?"

"Don't I always?" Sticking my tongue in her mouth, we

kissed like we did when we first met. I couldn't wait to get back

home to her. All the other times we fucked, it was because I beat

her ass and took it. This was the first time in a long time, we were

going to have sex because we both wanted to. Jumping in my car,

I headed to the warehouse. This shit better be an emergency or

me and Spade was about to have some problems.

When I pulled up, everyone was there except me. This

nigga better not come at me sideways in front of these lil niggas

or we were gone fight that shit out tonight and I would just have to deal with the consequences. When I walked in, you could tell

he was aggravated, but I didn't give a fuck.

"Tonight, something interesting happened. Someone was

bold enough to try and take my life. No nigga has ever shot at me,

but on tonight, they tried to air my ass out." The nigga paused for

dramatic affect. If I was a bitch, I would be rolling my fucking eyes.

How in the fuck was this an emergency? "Is there anyone in here

that would like to step up?" Everyone looked around at each

other trying to figure out what this nigga was trying to say.

"Are you insinuating that one of us shot at you?" The nigga

looked me dead in my eyes and for some reason, it shook me to

my core. I've never been scared of no nigga, but the look in his

eyes wasn't right and it caused me to start shifting in my sleep.

"I'm not insinuating anything. Bitches insinuate, I'm telling

you I know for a fact one of my own shot at me. When I left here, I

went straight to a chick's house. Nobody knew I was going there.

When I left her house, a mother fucker shot at me. The shit was

personal, and I only been to two spots. That tells me, one of you niggas followed me from here, and waited for me to leave. Now again, is anyone in here man enough to step the fuck up, or do I have to kill every nigga in here to get some answers?" My nerves kicked in because the nigga kept looking at me as if he was staring into my soul. When he grabbed his gun, I could barely swallow.

"Chris ass been talking about setting you up for a while now. I told the nigga it was suicide, but I ain't a snitch. All I'm trying to do is provide for my family and make money." This nigga Bruno talking about he ain't a snitch, when he did just that. Relieved that Spade finally took his eyes off me and walked over to Chris, my breathing turned back to normal.

"Hold on now Spade, I'm not gone lie. A nigga was mad because it felt like I'm constantly getting looked over. When I said that shit, I was pissed. I would never step to you. On King Leel I wouldn't do no shit like that." Out of nowhere, Spade slammed Chris down to the ground. Pulling his knife, he started carving a spade in the nigga's face.

"You not going to kill him first?" Spade never looked back at me and Chris was screaming at the top of his lungs. The shit was piercing my soul and it was hurting me. After he was done, we never got the chance to even react. Spade sliced the nigga throat so fast, I put my hands up to my shit.

"If a nigga think about taking me out, you will be Spaded. I will never give the nigga a chance to take me out. I AM NOT MY FATHER. ARE WE FUCKING CLEAR? No nigga will ever be able to run up on me and take me the fuck out. I'm giving any of you bitches the chance right now. Fair and square. If you got a problem with me, we can go head up right now. Man to man, gun to gun. Just know, I will not lose. Who the fuck wants it?" Everybody was shook silent, even me.

Not a nigga in there had anything to say. You could hear a deer piss on cotton at the moment. When Spade walked over to Bruno, I thought he was about to kill him as well. Hitting him with the gun, it looked like his jaw shifted.

"If you ever think a nigga trying to take me out and don't tell me, I will kill that family you're trying so hard to protect. If you know of a nigga that is against me and don't say shit, that tells me your ass against me as well. Are we clear?"

"Yeah boss man, we clear. My bad for that shit. Won't happen again."

"Now clean this shit up." Getting up, I damn near ran out of the warehouse. This nigga was coming unhinged and it might be in my best interest to get my shit together. The nigga shook me tonight, but I would never admit that shit. Nobody wanted to show up in the morgue with a signature Spade on their shit. Getting back in my car, I headed home. I didn't even want any pussy after that shit. It was too much on my mind and I'm sure my dick wouldn't work no way.

When I got in the house, La La was lying exactly like I told her to be. Not even removing my clothes, I laid down and turned my back. I could hear her sniffling, and the shit made me feel bad. There was no way I would be able to fuck her my shit was as limp as Biggie Smalls eye. My dick was dead like Kenny. She would just have to get over that shit. Tonight, my ass was going to sleep.

****

All day La La been walking around with an attitude, and I was over that shit. My ass damn near ran out of the door with no shower when Bruno told me we were going out tonight. I didn't even wait until later, I got dressed and took my ass to the warehouse until everybody was ready. We were supposed to hit up the Blue Note, but Spade wanted to go to the Skybox. After last night, everybody was scared to tell the nigga no.

They left before me because the numbers at one of my houses were short. Not wanting to piss that nigga Spade off, I stayed until every penny was accounted for. When I was done, I headed to the club to hang with my niggas. La La was mad at me for going out, but that attitude would go out the window when I got home and put this dick in her. That's all the fuck she needed, and she would be straight.

When I pulled up, I handed my keys to the bouncer and just walked in. It was perks to being the right hand and best friend of Spade. As soon as I walked in our section, I was ready to go to war. La La was here in this tight as dress and she knew I didn't want her nowhere near this nigga. I was about to drag her ass out of there until the girl on Spade's lap spoke up. Looking around, I could see the look on everyone's face like I was a weak nigga. Deciding to let it go, I sat down. I would deal with her ass when I got home.

Hearing Spade say his girl robbed him, pissed me the fuck off. That means La La helped her, and that nigga Spade might come at me about setting him up. This bitch had over stepped her bounds for the last time. Everybody was having a good time, but I couldn't stop thinking about different ways to drag La La when we got the fuck out of there.

Another thing that bothered me was this bitch that was with Spade. You would think they been together for a minute and this bitch was running shit. Maybe that's why his ass been acting like this lately. This hoe was in his ear trying to take my spot. This nigga was slipping being with a bitch that robbed him. You know what the fuck she here for, and she should have been dealt with accordingly. Yeah, that meant La La would have had to go to, but in this moment, it's fuck her.

I wasn't sure if I was pissed and seeing things, but it seemed like this bitch was stealing glances at Spade. It took everything in me not to choke this bitch up in the club. I was happy as fuck when Spade got up to leave. Everybody else followed suit, and you could see the fear on La La's face. Grabbing her hand, I tried to break her fingers I was squeezing so hard. The weak bitch was actually whimpering.

When we got in my car, I didn't say a word. I wanted my silence to shake her ass. You could tell she didn't want to get out of the car when we pulled up to the house. As soon as we walked in the door, I grabbed a chair and hit her bitch ass with it. She thought she was going to be around here fucking that nigga up under my nose, and I wasn't having that shit. Every time I hit her, I thought about the day I walked in Spade's house and she had her

ass in there naked. The bitch was trying to play me. They probably

been fucking this entire time. Hell, the baby could be this nigga's

child. I got so mad, I didn't realize I blacked out.

"Gino, I think I'm in labor." It was barely above a whisper,

but I heard her. Looking over at her body, I knew I couldn't take

her to the hospital. The way she was screaming, I knew she

wouldn't make it no way. Lifting her legs up, I saw the baby

coming out and I had to try not to throw up. Running to the back,

I got a towel and some scissors. Heading back to the kitchen, I got

some hot water and hoped that was enough. By the time I had

made it back to her, the baby was out and lying in between her

legs. In the movies, the doctors had to slap the baby for them to

scream. This lil nigga was screaming on his own. I cut the cord and

tried to get some of the blood off him.

"La La, here. You want your baby?" When she didn't

respond, I looked up at her. This bitch was laying there with her

eyes bucked open. I knew she was dead and the sad part is, I didn't even give a fuck. I laid the baby on the couch and got her

body. The baby couldn't turn yet, so I left to get rid of La La's

body. When I got back to the house, the baby looked blue and this

lil nigga was trying to die on me as well. Grabbing a blanket, I

wrapped him up and took him to the car. Looking over at him, his

ass was so white I convinced myself it had to be that nigga

Spade's baby.

When I pulled into the hospital, I took the baby inside. The

nurses grabbed him from me immediately. I'm assuming they

called the police because they were there Johnny on the spot to

talk to me.

"Sir, can you tell us what happened tonight?" My ass was

nervous because no nigga from the hood fuck with the police.

"When I got home, the baby was laying there, and his

mama was nowhere in sight. She had a few more weeks before

she gave birth. I don't know what happened, but I knew the baby

needed medical attention."

"Did you all have any enemies? Do she seem like the type that would leave her baby?" Thinking long and hard about what to say, I looked the officer dead in his eyes and lied.

"I thought she was just going through a phase. She continuously talked about her not wanting the baby. When we met, she was already pregnant, and I told her I would be the father. For some reason, she kept telling me I would eventually leave. I have no idea why she didn't want the baby, but I couldn't let him die. I'm sure it's a family out here that would love him." The officer raised his eyes at me.

"I thought you wanted the baby?"

"I did, as long as I was with the mother. She left me, so why would I raise her child? Not even a letter explaining what the fuck she was doing. This baby was left laying on my couch to die. I didn't even know what to do to save him. I'm not good enough to do this on my own."

"Do you know how to get in touch with her parents? Maybe she went there?" After I gave him her parent's info, I got the fuck up out of there. I did what I was supposed to do for the baby to live. I'm not about to raise it by myself and that nigga looking like Spade. That would be a slap in the face. I'm not sure if they still fucked, but I was convinced they was and that's all I needed.

Walking in the house, I cleaned up the blood that was on my floor. Pouring myself a drink, I realized how quiet and lonely the house was without La La. Trying to shake the thought that I may have fucked up, I continued to drink the entire bottle of liquor. After tonight, I was getting the fuck out of here. I needed a new spot to stay. It's like La La was haunting me in this bitch. She can have this mother fucker.

CHAPTER 14 SPADE

Seeing that nigga Gino come in the club acting a fool over that bitch pissed me off. It was a time and place for everything, and I don't do that embarrassing me in public shit. Pebbles wasn't even off the hook for the stunt she pulled. Jontanae saw me there and came and sat on my lap, I had every intention to tell her I was done with our lil fling when Pebbles came in showing her ass.

I'm not going to lie, the shit turned me on, but that's not the type of shit I do. I don't like all that ignorant shit out in public. My name carries too much weight and I wasn't about to have niggas thinking my shit wasn't in order. She thought when we got home, I was giving her this dick. Shorty had another thing coming. For some reason Pebbles think she can keep acting the fuck out on me and it won't be any consequences. I done let too much shit slide, but now that we fucking, all that shit was going out the window.

Same was about to go for Gino. I was more disappointed in him because he knew better. Whatever was going on between him and that bitch was between them, not the entire fucking club. These mother fuckers were running amuck and it was time for me to get this shit under wraps. Leaning over to Pebbles, I let her know what the deal is.

"Give your girl your keys. You going home with me tonight. If you try to make a scene acting like you don't wanna go, I will drag you out of this bitch. Just do what I asked and let's go." This was the second time she didn't fight me and listened to what I told her. Calling her friend over, she opened her purse and passed her the keys.

"If you scratch my shit, I'm gone scratch your ass. That's my baby and you better treat it as such." This girl didn't know how to talk without popping off.

"Girl ain't nobody gone do nothing to this car." Her friend walked off, and I pushed her forward for us to stand up. It was time to get the fuck up out of here. We headed to my car, and got

in.

"I was wondering if you had another car other than that

Porche. That's all the fuck you drive. Had me thinking you were a

broke as king pin. I like this color. I've never seen a Maserati in

white. Everybody always gets black." Even though I was tired of

her mouth, I laughed it off. She would change her tune once we

got to my place.

"For a mother fucker driving around in an old ass Benz,

you got a lot of shit to say. My Cayenne is my trap car. When you

get to my house, your lil ass ain't gone know who I am."

"My Benz is not that old."

"If you say so. Bun bun bun bunup." She laughed realizing I

was singing the theme song from Sanford and Son. It took us

about an hour to get to my house in St. Charles, IL. When we

approached my shit, her mouth was stuck open. My house was

the only one on the road and I knew my shit was legit. My pops

was ugly paid, when he died all his money went to me and my ol girl. If I didn't want to take over, I didn't have to. Even if she

wanted to say something smart, she couldn't. Just to add insult to

injury, I pulled into my garage, so she could see my other cars and

trucks. I had a mini car lot in my shit. Three bikes, a Rover, Bmw,

Bugatti, Phantom, Maybach, Benz, Porche, and Audi. Some I had

more of one just something different. In total I had fifteen

vehicles in here and that's not including my Porche truck.

"Why the fuck do you need so many cars? This shit is

ridiculous. You overcompensating for something?" Laughing, I

punched in my code and walked inside my house.

"You saw this dick, so don't act like you don't know what it

is. You think that's bad, wait until you see my house." Smacking

her lips, I let her inside. My shit was trimmed in fourteen karat

gold, and I had that bitch decked out. Seven bedrooms, five

bathrooms, a gym, indoor pool house, two kitchens, two front

rooms, a dining room, den, and indoor basketball court. It was a

lot for one nigga, but there was no way I was going to call myself

the King and don't live like one. Shit wasn't in my DNA. My pops

117

was a flashy nigga. You know what they say, the apple doesn't fall too far from the tree. To be honest, I think I was worse than he was. Walking her around the house, I showed her all the rooms one by one. When we got to my bedroom, I knew her ass was going to be speechless. I had my floor turned into an aquarium. Once you stepped inside, you were walking on a fish tank.

"You have got to be shitting me. This is some extra shit. A bitch had to decorate this house. Ain't no way a nigga this damn extra." Laughing, I took her to the last part of the house. The basement.

"Nobody has even seen this house, but my ol girl. I've never brought anybody here. No one knows where I live, and I would like to keep it that way. If you ever tell a mother fucker where I lay, you gone lay with the fish. I'm gone talk to your ass every night while you float in my floor." Opening the door to the basement, I let her in first. As soon as she was far enough in, I kicked her hard as fuck in the ass. The way she went sliding across the floor in them heels had me in tears. I don't see how her ass didn't break her ankles the way them shoes were leaning. Walking

towards the door I turned to face her.

"You gone stay down here until you learn some respect.

When you figure out who the fuck I am, maybe I'll let you out.

Until then, stay down here and think about that smart ass mouth

of yours." Before she could respond, I slammed the door and

locked it. I knew she was going to be pissed, but I didn't give a

fuck. I was King Spade and she was going to treat me as such. If

not, her ass was going to be the people under the stairs.

Heading back upstairs, I laughed as I pictured the look on

her face. I know she was trying everything under the sun to get

the fuck out of that basement. It wasn't possible, I made it that

way. No one could get in or out without my code. The shit was all

metal. After the shit with my father, I needed a safe room in my

house. I refused to go out the way that he did in my own shit.

I was fifteen years old and trying my best to prove to my

father that I was good enough to be a higher rank on his team. His

name carried weight, but he treated the people around him like shit. Even his family. Me and my moms had to endure the shit more than anyone else. No matter what we did, it was never enough. Walking to his office, I was determined to make him hear me. Knocking on his door, I waited for permission to enter.

"Come in." Putting on my strong face, I walked in and took a seat.

"Pops, I know you think I'm not ready for big responsibilities, but I am. Those niggas that robbed you, me and Gino took care of them. They didn't even see it coming. All I'm asking is for a chance to show you that I can do it. You trusting all these niggas to run your shit, but them mother fuckers hate your ass."

"Watch your fucking mouth when you are addressing me. I'm King Leel and you will treat me as such. You ain't did shit but create an enemy for yourself. If they come for you, I won't back you. Nobody told your dumb ass to go over there and do a mother fucking thing. You will never run my shit. You're too damn weak, just like your mother. Get out of my office, I have a meeting and

120

you're wasting my time." Leaving his office, I felt less than

nothing. I wanted to grab my gun and shoot his ass just to show

him who the fuck I was.

When I found out what Gino had up his sleeve, I felt his

pain. He treated all his workers like the help, but Gino was a

strong worker and I would hate for him to die trying to prove a

point. He was like me in so many ways, he just wanted to prove

who he was. My pops was just too stubborn to listen. Going in the

kitchen, I waited as our chef fixed me up something to eat. My

mother let a woman in and took her to my father's office.

I wondered who she was as I sat there and ate my plate.

Twenty minutes later, our front door flew off the hinges and ten

masked men came in our house with guns drawn. My gun was

upstairs, and I was pissed. One guy stayed with his gun trained on

us, while the others went towards my father's office. We heard the

gunshots and it was nothing we could do. They all walked back out

and the one with his gun trained on us left out behind them.

Me and my moms ran to my father's office and he was dead with his dick inside of the woman. My mother didn't even look surprised and I knew in that moment, I would never date a weak woman. This nigga was fucking another bitch in your house and she showed no emotion. I'm sure the woman set him up. That night taught me some valuable lessons. Never let another nigga get the chance to take me out, never let anyone know where you lay your head, and never fuck with a weak bitch.

"Hey Maria, I have a guest in the basement that is not to come out. Feed her a big ass breakfast, but you already know to be locked and loaded. I'll have some clothes for her as well. I'll leave them on the counter. Make sure she doesn't get out, or you will be terminated, and I don't mean fired." My House keeper and cook looked at me and knew what that meant. Walking up my long flight of stairs, I took my ass to sleep.

CHAPTER 15 SHVONNE

When I saw Spade's Maserati, I knew it was a lot about

him I didn't know. I thought I had his ass all figured out, but I

really knew nothing about his ass at all. When we pulled up to his

house, I knew I had him figured all wrong. I thought he was the

type that kept all his money saved up and stayed in an apartment

or some shit. This nigga mansion could feed a third world country.

I'm sure nobody knew this nigga was living like this or he would

have way more enemies.

A bitch was speechless looking at what he had. Me and

Bam thought we were living the life and our ass was considered

homeless compared to this shit. Taking it all in, a bitch could get

used to this. Putting it on him wasn't the word, I was gone have to

lay it the fuck down. There was no way I could let another woman

slip in and take what I wanted. This shit was going to be all mine.

When we got to the basement, I felt a sharp pain in my ass

and realized this nigga kicked me. Who the fuck kicks a bitch in the ass? It took everything in me not to bust my shit. My damn

heels were failing me, and I just knew I was going down. When I

finally got my composure, this nigga told me he was locking me

down here until I got some act right. Pissed wasn't the mother

fucking word when he locked that shit.

I liked the fact that he bossed up on me, but I damn sure

didn't want to be locked in a fucking strange ass basement.

Looking around, I was trying to find another exit strategy. After

thirty minutes of searching, I knew it was no way for me to get out

of here until Spade let me out. Grabbing my phone, I tried calling

La La so she could get Spade's number from Gino. When she

didn't answer, I threw that my phone across the room. How the

fuck you sleep with somebody and don't even have their phone

number?

Shaking my head, I was disappointed in my damn self. My

ass was so determined to throw him shade, I didn't even think to

ever get his number. Knowing I couldn't do shit tonight, I got in

the bed that was down there and laid down. People always said my mouth would get me in trouble, but I never expected some shit like this. All I could do was laugh. I laughed so hard a bitch started crying. One thing I knew was me and that nigga was going to war when he let me the fuck out of here. Closing my eyes, I tried my best to get some sleep.

****

Hearing the door open, I woke up ready to beat Spade's ass. Only to see some old ass lady walk in the door. This nigga must want me to be free sending her ass down here. Now I don't hit elders, but I was about to lay her old ass the fuck out. I needed to get out of this basement, and she was gone have to catch this fade. When I stood up, this old bitch pulled a gun on me.

"Mr. Spade said for me to use this if you try anything. I don't want to hurt you, but I don't want die. Please just sit down." This old bitch had to be shitting me.

"Quit playing with me and move out the way. We both know you are not about to shoot me." When I approached her, this bitch cocked it back and aimed at my ass like I was trying to steal her pussy.

"I'm going to ask you again nicely, please sit down and let me do my job." Reluctantly, I sat my ass down. Now that I was looking hard, this old bitch looked unstable.

"Tell Spade to bring his bitch ass down here and do his own dirty work. The fuck he send you for?"

"I'll deliver your message, but I'm going to need you to watch your mouth young lady. I don't know why Mr. Spade got you locked down here, but it may be because of how disrespectful you are. Nobody wants a woman that doesn't respect them. Oh, and just a heads up, Mr. Spade is really a nice guy. Don't push him though he has a mean streak like his daddy. You got a big breakfast here, and I got you some clothes, so you can shower. Think about what I said."

"Thank you." Granny left and locked the door behind her. Walking over to the table, my mouth watered when I looked at the food. I hope the shit tasted as good as it looked. When I took the first bite, I knew me and her were going to be good friends. As long as her old ass never pulled a gun on me again. Even though I don't like his method, I got the point he was trying to make. If I wanted all this to be mine, I was going to have to calm that shit down. I would always be me, but I've never been with anyone other than Bam. He didn't like the shit either, but he didn't go to these extremes so stop it.

Hearing the door open again, I continued to eat my breakfast like he wasn't coming in the room. Even though I really wanted to beat his ass, I chose to hold my composure. The cocky ass nigga came and sat across from me and smirked. It took everything in me not to get up and slap that bitch off his face.

"Good morning Pebbles."

"Hey." In my mind, I was screaming fuck you bitch ass nigga.

"I'm the king out here in these streets with a reputation to uphold. You are going to act like that when we are out in public. We get it, you're crazy and don't take no shit. Just remember, I don't either. Don't show your ass like that again. The shit ain't

lady like and you will not make me look weak out here to no

nigga. Are we clear?" In that moment, I realized what I had been

doing. I was never trying to make the next nigga think he was

weak, my ass just wanted him to understand that I wasn't.

"We're clear."

"Spade, what's your phone number?" Laughing, he pulled

his phone out.

"What's yours and I'll call it." I heard my phone ring and I

was glad my shit wasn't broke."

"Pebbles, since we're getting to know each other, what's

your real name?" It took me a second to decide whether or not I

wanted to give it to him, and he looked at me with a strange look.

Not wanting him to pull back, I decided to give it to him.

"Shvonne Lavigne."

"Nice to meet you Shvonne, I'm Jaleel Spade." Laughing at

his attempt to be normal, I grabbed my plate and walked behind

him. When he closed the door in my face and locked it, I was ready to say to hell with all that shit I just said and beat his ass.

This nigga was Hell and I was over this game he was playing.

Running to my phone, I called the number back that was on my

screen.

"Yes Shvonne."

"Why the fuck you lock me back in this basement? I get

the point. Now let me the fuck out of here."

"If you got my point, you wouldn't be talking to me like

that. In due time, you will get that mother fucker though. It's

either this or me beating your ass. Get in tune or get the fuck

gone." The nigga hung up in my face and I had to pick my lip up

off the floor. Grabbing my phone again, I dialed Halle's number.

CHAPTER 16 GINO

It's been a couple of days since the night I killed La La and this was the first time I had been out and about. I've been staying at a hotel and I needed to start looking for me a new place. This bitch was haunting me, and I couldn't sleep. I know I looked like shit, but I had to go check on the trap houses. The money didn't stop, and I didn't want Spade doing the most.

Making my rounds, picked up all the money that was owed and headed to the warehouse. The lot was empty, and I was happy about that shit. I didn't have to face Spade just yet and I could count this money and get the fuck out of here. Sitting down, I grabbed the money counter and went to work. I was so engrossed in what I was doing, I didn't even realize Spade was in the room.

"Did you know your bitch and her friends were robbing me?" I knew that shit was coming, I just hated that I was put in another position to get my ass shot the fuck up.

"You know I didn't. Why would I steal from myself? Make that make sense." You could tell my response aggravated him.

"Don't act like you don't have a disloyal trait my nigga. It was a time that you thought you should be higher than you were and wanted to take my pops out. I saved you because I knew the type of man my father was, but now your actions are showing me you just may be a disloyal nigga. Are you disloyal Gino?" Sweat popped on my forehead out of nowhere when I realized he was holding his gun.

"You know what it was with your father. He treated you the same way he did me. I could never take that shit back, but if you thought I was disloyal you wouldn't have kept me around all this time. I've never crossed you and I never will. Once you get that shit out of your head, we will be good."

"Look, if it walks like a duck and quacks like a duck, it's a disloyal nigga. You hid this bitch trying to act like you wasn't fucking her and you had a whole baby on the way. Then I get robbed by a group of bitches you couldn't find, but I rode down on them easy as hell. Come to find out the bitches that robbed

me, one of them is your baby mama. I get into a fight with you

and out of nowhere I get shot at. You tell me why the FUCK I

shouldn't think you moving funny nigga." When the gun laid

against my temple, thought about all the flawed shit I did and

regretted it. My ass was about to die and it was nothing I could do

to stop it.

"Don't make me have to question you again. You know I

never let a nigga get to me first. This is your last warning. Damn

shame when you can't even trust the closest nigga to you."

"For what it's worth, I'm not moving different. I hid La La

because I didn't want yall clowning me for staying with her ass. It

was nothing flawed about that." The nigga walked out like he ain't

here me talking to his bitch ass. Fuck him. I'm not about to keep

trying to explain to this nigga what the fuck it was. When he came

running back in the office, I thought the nigga changed his mind.

"Hurry up and put this shit up. The police just pulled up

nigga." We both grabbed the money and started throwing it in the safe. We barely finished before the officer walked in. My ass was

praying they were here to question Spade and not me. If he knew

what the fuck I did, his ass just might take me out.

"Hello Gino, we've been trying to find you, but you haven't

been home. We had to put a hit out on your license plate to find

you. I had a few more questions for you if you don't mind." Spade

was looking at me funny and I knew he thought it was on some

snitch shit. He would be even more disgusted to find out the

truth.

"I told you everything I knew."

"Was anyone else in your house? We're trying to figure

out who delivered the baby?"

"I already told you, when I got home the baby was laying

on the couch. I have no idea what happened. My concern was

saving the baby nothing more."

"You loved her though. Usually a person would

automatically think something bad happened. Not once did it

cross your mind that somebody could have taken her?"

133

"I already told you, she kept saying she was leaving. I assumed that's what she did. Is there anything to indicate that she didn't?"

"No it's not, I was just looking for clarity. Just in case you are wondering, the baby made it and her parents have him."

"That's good to know. He will be raised in a good home then. Thank you so much officer for updating me. If she contacts me, I'll call you."

"Thanks for your time." The officer left out, and I refused to look at Spade. I knew he had a million questions, but my ass was about to lie. No way I was going to give him the satisfaction of knowing I was jealous thinking she wanted him.

"Nigga tell me you didn't kill La La? What the fuck were you thinking Gino and why the fuck didn't you call the clean up crew?"

"You know we don't give second chances. I don't know why you ain't killed the chick you fucking with. You coming at me thinking I'm flaw, but you know she robbed you and ain't did shit.

134

La La ass played me. Stealing info and taking it to them bitches. She had to go because I couldn't trust her. How the fuck I was supposed to know she wouldn't rob us again, or turn us in to the police? That shit had me spooked that somebody who was carrying my baby could rob me." My lie must have worked because it looked like he understood my reason.

"You still should have called the clean up crew to do it the right way. I'm not gone tell you what you should and shouldn't have done, but I don't think they would have done it again. In your case, I can understand the betrayal you felt. My situation is different, she didn't know who the fuck I was when they robbed the house. Next time, give me a heads up when you do some shit like this."

"My bad, you right. She had to go though. I'm not laying up with a bitch I don't trust."

"That's your right. I'm going to tell the girls that she is missing. No way I'm telling my girl you killed her friend. I would advise you to do the same."

135

"Aight bet." When he left out, I was finally able to breathe. Now that I had Spade back on my side, the show could go on. Locking up, I left the warehouse. I needed to find me a new place to live. No one would know where I stayed at, because I may need to hide out in the future.

I was losing control and it was time for me to get a grip on this shit. You could tell the police didn't believe the bullshit ass story I gave them. Grabbing my phone, I called my homie at the car lot. I was going to need a new car with some dealer plate. This was the last time I would allow myself to be this accessible.

CHAPTER 17 SPADE

This nigga Gino was out of control, but I understood his reasoning. Normally, that would have been the same shit I would have done. If you can't trust a bitch, you kill a bitch. That's always been my motto and that's why Gino's time was coming to an end. Him killing La La gave me a lil faith in his ass, but it was too many what ifs. Heading back to the house, I knew I had to tell Pebbles. She would be happy to finally be out of the basement.

When I walked in my house, I headed downstairs. She looked tired and broken. I haven't been down here since breakfast the first morning she was there. I'm sure she would feel some type of way, but I needed her to get that shit through her head. When she didn't look up, I started to feel bad.

"Shvonne get up. I need you to shower so we can get out of here." Finally raising her head, you could tell she was trying to see if I was serious. Giving her a chance to show me she was trust worthy, I left out and didn't lock the door. I waited upstairs for her, giving her time to get ready. An hour later, she came upstairs.

My baby's hair was curly again and I loved that shit like that. It

made her look innocent as hell. My baby was rocking the hell out

of her Givenchy outfit and Sneakers I got for her. I'm guessing I

got the right size because it was hugging the shit out of her.

"Where we going?" A nigga wanted her to calm down, but

I didn't want to break her. Her voice was dull as hell. It's like she

left her personality in the basement.

"I don't have nothing planned. Just want to get you out of

the house. Plus, we need to talk." All she did was nod and waited

for me to get up. "Come on." Going into the garage, I jumped in

the Bugatti and gave her the keys. Her eyes lit up and it was nice

to see some spark in her again. Guiding her to one of the parks, I

got we got out and started walking. Grabbing her hand, I told a lie

for the first time in my life.

"Baby, we can't find La La. She gave birth to her baby, but

when Gino got home she was nowhere to be found. She has been

gone since day after the club. We are looking for her though."

Snatching her hand away, she turned to face me. You could see

the fire in her eyes, but she didn't want to go back in the

basement, so her tone was calm and in a whisper.

"You know Gino did something to her. That girl would not

leave her baby. You have to do something Spade." That was the

one thing I hope she wouldn't ask of me.

"Shorty that shit between them. You may not like what

that nigga does to her, but she keeps going back. We can't get in

that shit."

"You know that's not it. I've never gotten involved, but he

did something to her. This is different." You could see the tears in

her eyes, but it looked deeper than what she was saying.

"I can't get involved in that shorty. It's not my business."

Seeing the disappointment in her eyes made me feel bad.

Grabbing her to me, I lied again to try and comfort her. "Let's just

hope she okay. The baby is with her parents. I'm sure she will

come back for her baby. Maybe she just wanted to get away from

that nigga." Nodding her head, I knew she was putting her trust in me. Looking around the park, I saw we were the only ones out there. I sat on the bench and pulled her down in my lap. Kissing on her neck, I unbuttoned her jeans while I had her focused on my tongue. Sliding them down enough to get my dick in, but not fully expose her I slid my dick out.

"You want this dick?" She shook her head fast as hell, but I wouldn't put it in. "Use your words Shvonne."

"Yes Spade. Please put it in." Pulling her down on my dick, I let her do her thing. Either she couldn't adjust to my size this way, or her ass couldn't ride no dick. Grabbing her by her hair, I pulled her back to me. Sucking on her neck, I used my other hand to play with her clit.

"Ride this dick like you want it. You don't have to go crazy, just precise." Me playing with her clit must have worked, because she slowly started riding. Once she got the hang of it, she had my toes popping in my Balenciagas. "Fuck. Just like that baby." How the fuck she knew how to tighten her muscles when she was just riding with no rhythm was beyond me, but that shit was bringing

140

tears to my eyes. Every time she went up, it's like she was

suctioning my shit. She was trying to snatch my soul and my nut at

the same damn time. Speeding up the motion, I continued to rub

her clit and sucking her neck at the same time.

"Cum on this dick baby. Cum for me." Biting her neck, I

flicked her clit at full speed and she went crazy.

"Fuuuucckkk. I'm cumming baby." Her body convulsed,

and she came all over my shit. As soon as she stopped shaking, I

pushed her off me. Pointing my dick at the grass, I let my kids play

hide and seek. Putting my dick up, I waited for her to fix her

clothes as well before I pulled her back to my lap.

"I'm sorry for leaving you down there that long. I wasn't

trying to take away your personality, I just wanted you to

understand you have to respect me. Especially in public."

"I get why you did it, but don't do that shit no more. You

had that old ass lady down there trying to pull a trigger and her

arthritis was acting up."

"Mary would have killed your ass in a minute. Don't underestimate her."

"Only thing she killing is a bottle of ben gay. Stop your shit." We both laughed at her lame attempt at a joke.

"It's good to see you back. I don't know your story, but I'm tired of seeing you so sad all the time. You think you be hiding that shit, but your eyes tell it all. I'm rough around the edges, but I'm that nigga. Let me give you what you're missing. Let me show you what the fuck happiness looks like. Let a nigga put a smile on your face." She gave me a weak ass smile, but I hoped she was hearing me.

"Okay." Grabbing her, I wanted to show her I was serious. Walking back to my car, I let her drive again. This time, I directed her to my mother's house. I didn't tell her where we were going, but I hoped she would appreciate the gesture. When we pulled up, she looked at me like I was crazy.

"I know you don't have two big ass houses. What is wrong with you? As skinny as you are, you sure need a lot of damn space. This is just too damn much. Let me have one of these

mother fuckers shit."

"This my ol girl's house. If you want a house, I'll get you

one. Or you can just come to my shit." Her ass almost looked

terrified when I said that shit and I knew I was moving too fast.

"Why would you bring me here without telling me? Do I

look okay? Did you fuck my hair up?"

"You look fine Shvonne calm your ass down. I'm trying to

show you that I'm serious. Now come on." Reluctantly, she got

out of the car and walked to the door. Ringing the bell, I held her

hand trying to calm her while I waited. My moms opened the door

and looked shocked as fuck.

"Well hello son. Who is this?" She was staring at Pebbles

like she was a damn ghost.

"Ma this is Shvonne, baby this is my mama Ms. Janice."

"Nice to meet you Ms. Janice." My moms gave some weird

as smile and we walked inside the house. I was confused why she

was acting like this. It's probably because I have never brought anybody over here. Not even one of my guys. Nobody knew

where either of us lived. I didn't even think to ask my moms was

she okay with the shit first.

"You cooked? I smell food." When she gave me the death

look, I knew shit was about to go left.

"Don't play with me nigga. Why the fuck you bring this girl

to my house? I don't know her and I'm assuming you don't either

since you never mentioned her. Then have the nerve to come in

here smelling like pussy. If you don't get your dumb ass out my

house. Baby girl, no disrespect, but forget my mother fucking

address. Don't ever come here again, with or without my son."

Shocked wasn't the word. I knew my moms was outspoken when

it came to other people, but I wonder why she wasn't this feisty

when it came to my dad.

"Excuse me." I prayed Pebbles didn't disrespect my mama

even though she wouldn't be wrong. It was no way I could date a

girl that cursed my moms out.

"You heard what the fuck I said. I can look at you and tell you ain't right. Something off about your ass and I'm going to advise you to stay the fuck away from my son." Before Pebbles could respond or hit my mama, I snatched her out the door.

"Wait for me in the car please." Walking back into my mama house, I was ready to go the fuck off.

"What the fuck was that shit? You had to know she meant something to me if I brought her here, why would you do that?"

"Because you dumb as hell if you trust that girl. Her eyes tell it all and it's something about that bitch that ain't right. If you bring her over here again, your ass will be on the porch. Big ass wig on her head. Never trust a bitch that thinks she's Tina."

"Everybody not like your damn husband. I get that you have a phobia about strangers being in your house, I do too. But you know what you just did was fucked up. Not once did you ever stand up to dad, but you can judge every damn body else. Get your shit together and fix your damn wig why you in here talking. How the fuck you calling somebody Tina and your ass in here

145

looking like Patty?" Flapping my arms like Patty Labelle used to

do, I walked out and slammed her door. I was pissed to see

Pebbles left my ass. She done fucked up my storm out now I gotta

go back in here looking stupid. Turning around, I knocked on the

door.

"What the fuck you want?"

"Ma, I need to borrow your car. She left me." My mama

laughed in my face.

"Get your ass off my porch and run your dumb ass home.

Gone Forrest. Stupid is as stupid does looking ass. I hope them

sock looking ass shoes comfortable. Around here wearing footies

thinking you cute." When she slammed the door in my face I was

ready to beat Pebbles ass. I know she was in there having a good

laugh at my expense. Sitting down on the porch, I knew she would

kill me if I called someone to come get me and I would regret it as

well. Hearing her door open, the keys hit me in the head before I

could turn around.

"Get your nasty ass off my porch. Gone have my steps smelling like gold digging pussy. I want a new car too since you think it's okay to talk to your mama like that." She slammed the door again, and I walked to her car. I couldn't wait to find Pebbles. I had a good mind to send her ass back to the basement for a month.

This girl was going to be the death of me. Even though I told her to turn her crazy down, my slow ass was turned on because she was crazy enough to leave me in my own shit. She better had took her ass back to the house. On the way home, the only thought that crossed my mind was I wonder if she knows how to give head.

CHAPTER 18 SHVONNE

That nigga Spade was looking sexy as fuck when I came out of the basement. His hair needed to be redone, but his dreads still looked sexy on him. I don't know what kind of gold he had in his mouth, but them shits was shining when he smiled at me. He was in a Ralph Lauren jogging suit, so I couldn't see his tats. Normally a small guy wouldn't look this sexy to me, but he wasn't the bony type of skinny. He had some muscles on his frame. I just wanted to climb on his lap and kiss him for hours. Those lips looked they could eat the skin off some pussy.

My ass was ready to do all kinds of nasty shit to him until he told me about La La. I knew in my heart that Gino did something to her. I hoped like hell Spade was right when he said she ran away, but I knew that wasn't likely. If she had took the baby, I might have had some type of hope. My ass never wanted to go to the club again. Bam died at the club and La La went missing after going to the club. That shit was jinky as fuck. You could tell he felt me going into a depression and he knew just

what to do to bring me back. I've never had sex in public, but that

shit was intense as fuck. After that shit, all I wanted to do was go

back to the house and fuck until tomorrow. That nigga had some

good dick, but I needed to keep him focused on me. When you

give a bitch room to get in, they will come in and take over. Not

on my fucking watch they won't.

My pussy was still jumping, and this nigga done pulled up

to his mama house. Who in the fuck brings you to their mama

house and don't tell you. I would have dressed up or something.

Well, that was until I met her ass. The way she was talking, I

should have come over in my Tims and brass knuckles. That bitch

was disrespectful as hell. Spade knew I was about to beat her ass

and got me the fuck out of there.

I knew he would be mad, but I had to get the fuck away

from her or I would have ran back in her shit. I've never had

someone talk to me like I was the gum stuck on their Payless

specials. Especially not some old ass mother fucker who didn't

149

know how to let her son go. Trying my best to remember where

he lived, I drove back. His ass could stay over there, or she could

bring his ass home. Old ass bitch looked like she smoked squares

all day while looking out the window. There was no way me and

her could ever get along. If he ever takes me around her again,

she was going to need a walker after I beat her ass. Before Spade

got back and tried to put me in the basement again, I decided to

cook for him. My intentions were to soften his ass up.

"Maria, what kind of food do we have in here? I want to

cook for Spade, but I don't know what he likes or what's here."

"I was about to prepare him some chicken and shrimp

alfredo. All the stuff is here you just have to prepare it. Are you

sure you want to do this? Mr. Spade is very picky with his food."

"Yes, I got it. Matter fact, you can take the night off. I'm

sure it's something you want or need to do. Don't worry, I will tell

him I made you leave if he gets mad."

"Trust me, I'm definitely going to blame you if he goes off.

I hope you guys have a nice night. He will appreciate the effort."

"I hope so." Washing my hands, I got started. Grabbing a skillet, I poured some olive oil in the pan, so I could cook my chicken. Once I got everything going, I looked in the refrigerator and was pleased to see Maria had some wine. Pouring me a glass, I sipped while I waited on my chicken to cook. I heard the garage open and I knew it was Spade. When he walked in the door, he looked pissed. Until he saw I was cooking, then his face softened.

"Why would you leave me? I went in there going the fuck off and stormed my ass out and I had to go back in and beg for her car." I tried my best not to laugh, but the shit was funny as hell.

"Baby, if I had stayed, I would have beat your mama ass. I had to get the fuck off her property. Her mouth disrespectful as hell, but my hands disrespectful as fuck."

"You look like the type to fight old bitches to make yourself look good. What you in here cooking and where is Maria? If this shit nasty you going back in that basement."

"I gave her the night off, and nigga I can cook. It ain't my fault you used to dating Ramen Noodle bitches. Now go sit your ass the fuck down and let me do my thing." Spade walked up to me and kissed me on my neck. A bitch almost said fuck this food and went to get some dick. That was going to come later though. When I hooked up the shrimp, I used this recipe La La gave me. She cooked some one day and the shit had me slobbing it was so good. Just thinking about her made me sad. Ironically, it started me to think about my best friend Tiana. Grabbing my phone, I called her.

"Heeeyyy best friend. What you doing?"

"Hey girl. Out here trying to look for a come up. My rent past due and you know I ain't trying to get put out of my shit."

"Fuck all that. I'm going to buy you a ticket and you can come live out here with me. Well not with me because I have a roommate, but we will figure something out."

"Don't play with me bitch. If you serious I'm going to pack my shit right now and sit at the airport until you send the ticket."

"I'm dead ass. I'll do it when we hang up and send you the info. I can't wait to see you."

"Thank you so much Pebbles. I'm going to pack now."

Hanging up, I set up her ticket and sent her the information. It felt

good to have my best friend coming. We were about to fuck this

city up. Now I needed to see if Spade knew someone that could

have a place ready by tomorrow.

Waiting until I was done with dinner, I wanted to butter

him up first. Fixing it making it look pretty as hell, I grabbed him a

soda and fork. Walking to his office, I placed the plate on his desk.

When he looked up, he looked stressed as hell. You could tell he

was carrying the weight of the world on his shoulders.

"It smells good shorty." Grabbing the fork, he tasted it and

then dug in. "Yeah, you did your thing. Guess you didn't want to

be in that basement after all."

"Fuck you. Listen, I need you to make some calls for me.

My best friend is coming to live here, but it's no space in my

condo. I need to find her a place by tomorrow." Not responding,

he continued to eat. Taking that as a no, I got up and decided to

try and make some calls myself.

"Where you going Shvonne? Sit down. I'm not ignoring you the food good as fuck and I wanted to be done before I continued. You know your ass like to fight and I didn't want my shit to get cold. By the time I drop kicked your ass in the basement, my shit would have been fucked up. Now that I'm done, here is my proposition. You stay here and let her stay at your condo."

"We haven't been dating that long. Do you think that's a good idea?" Grabbing me to him, I felt how hard his dick was and the shit turned me on.

"I'm addicted to that pussy which means I'm going to be at your shit or you're going to be here every night. I need to feel that shit squeezing my dick every night. May as well stay here. Let me take care of you. If we get into it, this house is big enough for us to be here for days and not see each other. Besides, it's always the basement."

"Okay, we can try it. Just know if you be on some bullshit, that old Pebbles coming the fuck back. I been trying this new way

154

for you, but your wrinkled ass mama almost brought that old

thang back."

"Come here, I got something to show you." Jumping up, I

got excited. I loved surprises, it made me feel like a kid. My ass

practically on his heels. When he opened the garage door, it was

another Bugatti sitting there with a bow on it.

"I know the fuck you didn't. Spade, did you buy me a car?

Tell me you did not buy me a mother fucking Bugatti."

"Naw, that's for my mama. I was trying to ask you do you

think she will like it?" The dumbest look came across my face and

I felt like shit.

"Oh. Yeah it's nice."

"Fix your face, it's your car." His ass started laughing, and I

slapped the shit out of his ass. It was reflex, but now I was

regretting it. His ass better not put me in that damn basement.

Grabbing me by my hands, he slammed me on the hood of the

car.

"Didn't I tell you to keep your fucking hands to yourself. I'm too yellow for all that shit. Keep trying me, your ass gone live in that damn basement. Now, come here and suck my dick." Laughing, I walked over to him while his ass tried to sing. "I got my dick sucked in a new Bugatti."

"Spade, we gotta go get my Benz so I can park my shit in here too. I want more than one car in this bitch too."

"I sold that old ass Benz the next day. You always talking shit, but you riding around in a Benz that's square shaped. I got you though. I'll get you an everyday car." I'm usually good at hiding my emotions, but my face twisted up and the tears began to fall. Taking off running, I went to one of the rooms and balled up. It was the only thing I had that kept me attached to Bam. He bought me that car and now it was gone. Crazy thing is, I wasn't crying from sadness, I was crying from anger. What gave him the fucking right? Spade had this shit twisted.

CHAPTER 19 SPADE

I thought Pebbles would be happy, but the minute I told her I got rid of the Benz, everything in her changed. I needed to find out this girl's past. She was holding on to something and I couldn't compete with that. As long as she was stuck there, she would never let me in and heal her. The shit falls on me though, I should have been trying to figure out who she was and what she been through. My ass was too busy trying to get her to be what I wanted, I never stopped to think that maybe it was a reason she was that way.

It took me a while to find her. My ass had to go through damn near every room to find out where she took off to. Her ass would pick the room furthest from us. That tells me she really didn't want me to find out her. When I walked in, she was balled up and screaming like someone snatched her soul. To hear her crying like that told me I fucked up bad. Even though I had no idea what I did, my ass felt bad as fuck. All I wanted to do was make

157

her happy. I wanted to show her that since she was with me, she wouldn't want for anything and didn't need to be out here stealing money. How the fuck did that turn into this shit? Thinking back on it, she always went into a depressed ass state. Giving her time to calm down, I waited until she wasn't screaming to say something.

"Shvonne, look at me." It took her a minute, but she finally looked up. "What is going on and I don't want a general ass answer. Maybe we should have done this shit day one, but now it's time for this conversation. I need to know your past, where you come from, and why you keep going into this depressed ass state."

"My boyfriend was killed some years back. The car was the last thing he gave me, and you gave it away. Sometimes something just reminds me of him, and I end up crying I try not to think about it, but sometimes I can't help it." Nodding my head, I could understand that.

"It's hard moving on, but you have to do it for your sanity. My dad was killed while I was there, but I can't live my life stuck in that mind frame. You couldn't hold on to that car forever. He's in your heart and that's all that matters. Nobody can ever take that from you."

"Somebody already did. Look, I just want to be alone. When I get like this, it's best to just be by myself. I'll be good, I just have to focus." This was the type of shit that pissed me off.

"Focus on what? Crying. You sound real dumb right now. We're about to be living together and we can't even have a real conversation. You need to grow the fuck up. Death happens, we deal with it and move on. Just know, if you my bitch, you not about to be in here crying over another nigga every damn day. Fix yourself up, when I get back I still want some head and I don't like snot in my shit." Getting up, I walked out. I was trying to go off on her, but she was pissing me off. Every time shit got real, she turned into a straight bitch.

Jumping in my car, I headed to the store in the city. I needed a fucking drink if I was going to be dealing with Pebbles. This was the type of shit that make you want to fuck another bitch just for peace of mind. When I walked in the door, it was a group of girls standing there waiting on their order.

"Heeyy Spade. You looking good boo."

"And you still looking like section eight." The bitch giggled like she thought I was just being funny.

"You so silly. When you gone come over my house and let me show you what a real woman is like."

"I'll come over when your rent is more than fourteen dollars." Walking out, I didn't even want to wait on my liquor. The bitch was irritating the fuck out of me.

"Spade, why do you have to always be so damn rude. I've been trying to get with you for years. Come on, let me show you how good I can make you feel." The bitch grabbed my dick and damn near pinched my meat off. Before I could break her wrist, pebbles came flying out of nowhere and drop kicked the girl in the back. When I say flying, I literally mean her ass was flying. Looking like the yellow power ranger. The girl fell into me causing us both to fall to the ground. Even though I was pissed my Gucci shirt got dirt on it, I was happy Pebbles was here to beat this thirsty bitch up.

"Pebbles, beat her ass and you better win too." That was all I needed to say, and Pebbles went crazy. I almost felt bad for the girl until her friends ran outside and tried to help. I don't fight bitches, but I wasn't letting mine get jumped. I gave all her friends a sleepy time punch and let Pebbles whoop her a few more minutes. Once I was over it, I grabbed Pebbles and drug her back to the car.

"How the fuck you knew where I was?" Her neck started rolling and her lips were popping and I had to fight myself not to laugh.

"Knew? Nigga I followed you. I got dick in trouble radar. When you left the house, that shit started going off and I knew your hoe ass was on the way to fuck another bitch. So I followed your ass. Just remember that shit the next time you go scrounging

through the hood looking for friendly pussy."

"Did you not hear me tell you to beat her ass? Bitch

grabbed my dick and almost took the skin off. Now take your ass

to the house."

"Fuck no. I'm not going in that basement, you told me to

fight her. That shit on you, maybe you need to go in the fucking

basement." Smiling, I was glad to know she was scared of that

shit. Maybe her ass would act right.

"Go the fuck to the house, you not going in no damn

basement. I still want my dick sucked and my shit hard as fuck

from watching you handle business. If I beat you there, I get that

booty hole too." She must don't like it in the ass, Pebbles jumped

in the car and damn near ran my foot over she took off so fast.

Laughing, I jumped in my car. Man this bitch had me gone.

As soon as I pulled up, I laughed when I saw her car.

Mother fucker even left skid marks in my damn drive way. She

didn't know it yet, but her ass was coming out here to clean that shit up. If it didn't come up, her ass was about to be Bob the

builder around this bitch. When I walked in the door, I was about

to curse her ass out for how she did my driveway, but she was

sitting at the island in the kitchen waiting on me sucking a

popsicle. The way she was doing that shit had my dick busting out

of my jeans. She already had the sexiest lips I ever seen on a bitch,

but damn.

"You sucking that shit like you ready to deep throat this

dick."

"Naw, I'm sucking this shit trying to practice. I don't want

you to throw me in the basement for having mediocre head. You

know you used to fucking ratchets, them bitches can suck quarter

out of a piss hole." She was bat shit crazy, but that's exactly how I

liked her ass. We would work on everything else along the way,

for now, I just wanted to show her that she could be loved again.

CHAPTER 20 GINO

Everything has been going smooth between me and Spade lately. I've been actually doing my job and he has been trusting me a lot more. It's a lot that has been done over the years, but it seems like everything was cool. Sometimes, all you had to do was your job and shit will go the way you want it. Mother fuckers respect you more when you not fucking up.

Going through the money one more time, I made sure the count was right. Putting it in the safe, I left it for Spade to issue it out where it goes. Leaving out the office, I saw Bruno and them just hanging out when I know they had work to do. If it was Spade that had walked in, they ass would be on the way to the incinerator.

"You telling me, there is nothing out there to be done? All the drugs are issued out, all the shit is bagged up, and all money is accounted for at the traps? WHY THE FUCK ARE YOU JUST SITTING AROUND LIKE IT'S NOT WORK TO BE DONE?"

164

"We were just taking a break Spade Jr. On King Leel niggas be around here sucking nut sacks. Mother fucker was just on the verge of getting Spaded and now he wanna be in here running shit." This nigga Bruno thought he was funny as hell, but Spade wasn't here to save his ass.

"You got a lot of mouth for a nigga here with no back up. When Spade isn't here, who the fuck you think is in charge. As the nigga in charge I think your time done fucking expired. Who in the fuck gone save you now lil nigga?" Grabbing my gun, I pointed it at his head. How I know these niggas don't respect me, the bitch ass mother fucker pulled his and pointed it at me. He would have never did that shit to Spade.

"What the fuck yall doing?" Spade walked in, but neither of us dropped our guns. "I don't like repeating myself."

"Bro this slip and slide nut sucker came out here talking shit cus we were taking a break and shit. Nigga trying to be you so bad the shit made my balls itch. Anybody that knows me, know I hate itchy balls. Nigga pulled his gun, so I pulled mine." You could see Spade thinking it over, if this nigga went against me we were about to have a full shoot out in this bitch.

"Gino is my right-hand man. If I'm not here, then he is next in charge. If he told you to get back to work, then that's what the fuck you do. You shouldn't be taking a break no damn way, your ass just got here. Gino, don't pull no gun attempting to take out no mother fucker I hand picked. Hit me up, and I'll deal with his ass. You know this my lil nigga." Putting my gun away, I was happy he let them niggas know what was up. I just hated he told them I couldn't touch they ass.

"Well you better get his ass in check. Nigga pop off like that at me again, I'm gone shoot his lips off. You know you wouldn't play that shit, why would you expect me to?" Spade's expression changed, but it wasn't anger. You could tell he agreed with what I said.

"You right, but I'm asking you off the strength of me because that's my lil nigga. If a problem occurs just hit me up. If the shit is too far left or he did some real fucked up shit, I won't stop you from doing what you have to do. As a man, I understand not wanting to be disrespected. Don't think I don't get that, but that's my lil nigga. Run me that solid." Appreciative of his tone, I agreed to that.

"Bet. I can do that."

"Come take a drive with me." That shit came out of nowhere and it had me thinking was that shit all a front. Was he baiting me to get me by myself to take my ass out? Spade wasn't a scary nigga, if he wanted me dead he would do it here. Relaxing some, I walked out with him and got in his white Audi. He hardly ever drove this car, but it was nice as hell.

We ended up at Carmichael's Trap house, and I wondered what the fuck we were doing there. This nigga worked for us, but we didn't fuck with him like that. His attitude was bad for business, so we never affiliated ourselves with him. Looking to Spade for answers, he laughed because he knew what I was thinking.

"You still pissed off and I figured you need to blow off some steam. I was gone come lay these niggas out myself, but I figured I'll let you tag along to release some of that anger. These niggas popping off about how they about to be running shit, now they about to be running Hell." Grabbing my gun, I was down to blow some steam. Walking inside, Carmichael was shocked to see us.

"What brings yall down here with the common folk?" Spade didn't even answer the nigga, he just started shooting. When I saw he didn't come to talk, I did the same thing. Once everyone was down, Spade walked around the room carving a Spade in their faces. Just as we were about to walk out, a lil ass Tequila Taco Bell dog ran out barking. Spade shot him and carved his signature on him as well.

"You're sick as fuck. The dog nigga?" Shaking my head, I walked out.

"It's just one of them days. I was in a killing kind of mood and now I'm good. You straight? Go get you some pussy and I'll see you tomorrow. Pebbles friend coming today, and we have to

get her settled in.

"Is she cute? Hook me up if she is." This nigga laughed in

my face.

"You just killed her friend. Pebbles ain't going at gun

point."

"Whatever nigga." We drove back to the warehouse

listening to Dedication Six By Lil Wayne. As soon as we pulled up, I

got out and got in my shit. If Bruno was still in there, it would be

better for me to leave. Stopping at the store before I went home, I

went in to get me some swishers.

"Heyyyyy Gino. How you doing?" Looking up, I saw

Jontanae and she was looking fine as fuck.

"What's up Nae. You looking good girl."

"Good enough to eat?" That comment threw me off

especially since she used to fuck with Spade. It sounded like she

was choosing and a nigga like me wasn't equipped to turn down

good pussy.

169

"Girl stop playing with me before I give you what you looking for. You know damn well you not trying to fuck with a nigga like me and I thought you was riding Spade's jock."

"Me and Spade are done and I'm looking for some new dick. My kids gone for tonight and that shit don't happen often. You want to come over?" Thinking about it, Spade did fuck my bitch why I can't fuck his?

"I'll follow you." The shit may be wrong, but it was about to feel right. Jumping back in my whip, I followed behind her. My mind was telling me not to go, but Spade ain't never been pressed over a bitch. My dick wouldn't allow me to turn around, so I let the chips fall where they may.

CHAPTER 21 SHVONNE

Now I said luxury apartments, I'm young and I'm heartless. There's a bitch that's in my vision, that bitch is a target. Lawyer is a Jew, he gone chew up all the charges. Don't matter if you fuck with me I get money regardless.

"Bitch you don't feel this shit. Cardi B killed this Bickenhead shit. I don't give a fuck what they say about her I fuck with that bitch." Halle was looking at me like I was crazy because I was all worked up.

"That's because you always trying to kill a bitch. Who the fuck you got in your vision you trying to take out? It's somebody because your ass always mad as hell." She was always trying to play doctor and shit. Bitch took one Psychology class and now she around here acting like Dr. Suess.

"Girl I am not trying to kill nobody. My ass just in a good mood because shit is going how it should be. Me and Spade are straight, and a bitch been getting more dick than this pussy could take. Why the fuck wouldn't I be in here singing and dancing. It's been a long time since I been able to stand around and dance and shit. Girl let me be great."

"Well shit I'm with you then. Let's get lit. When your best friend come in, we should go out tonight. I hope she nicer than your ass though since you just gave my ass a roommate."

"Clubs ain't for me I don't think. Every time I go, something happens."

"You can't think like that. We're going to have a good time, and nothing is going to happen. They haven't found a body for La La, so maybe she really did leave that nigga."

"That's what Spade keeps telling me. I hope yall right and we can go out tonight. Just know, if some shit pop off, I'm beating that mustache off your face."

"Can I wear your Fendi bag tonight? I got this dress that would match it perfectly. I'm trying to be fly like your ass."

"No."

"Damn bitch you not gone laugh or nothing? Just no?"

172

"Yeah, we don't do that. I'm not even about to let you start thinking we can do that shit. I pay entirely too much money to be out here acting like Lending Tree.com Let's get that clear. Wear what you can afford. Your fly should match your pockets, not mine."

"Sometimes I wish you wasn't so scary, I would beat your ass. You so damn disrespectful friend. Your ass don't give a fuck what you say out your mouth. Keep being mean to me imma tell Spade to put your ass back in that damn basement." I couldn't do shit but laugh. When I told her that shit, she was on the fucking floor. I damn near got mad she laughed so damn hard."

"Let's go get something to eat. I got a taste for Ronnie's Steak House. It shouldn't be packed this time of day. If we hurry up, we should be able to get a table."

"You know a bitch like me can always eat. I didn't get these thighs eating lettuce. Since you got this new fancy ass car, you driving bitch." Leaving out, we headed downtown to go get us some good ass steak. I've been cooking and giving Maria a lot of time off, but today, I just wanted somebody else to cook for me. I

needed to finish packing and I didn't have time to be out here

trying to cook.

Valeting my car, we headed inside. The food started calling

my name as soon as I walked in the door. A bitch stomach did the

Milly Rock and I danced my way all the way to the counter. I

couldn't wait to get some of this good ass food. California didn't

have food like this. The shit had a different taste. Before I could

even get my shit, I looked over and saw the bitch I beat up in the

club all cozy in this bitch with Gino. Tapping Halle, I pointed over

to the corner and her mouth hit the floor. Not being able to let it

go, I walked my ass right on over.

"Hey 2 Pac. I see you found another money bag huh? Yall

look cozy. Have you been out looking for La La Gino, or just laid up

with this bitch while your baby mother missing?"

"Who the fuck is 2 Pac? My name is Jontanae."

"You know 2 Pac. He sung I get around."

LOCKED DOWN BY HOOD LOVE

"Round and round, round and round." When Halle started singing it, we both started doing the dance. The bitch was pissed that we started laughing and high fiving.

"Cute, but if you don't mind, I'm on a date. Last I checked, you're with Spade, so I don't see the problem."

"The problem is, our friend is missing and he all up in here with your ass. Don't try to be cute, it will take too fucking long. You should just get the fuck up before we remove you ourselves." Halle was saying a whole bunch of we's, but I wanted to know if she could fight. The girl didn't move, and Halle hit her. It wasn't as hard as I would have done, but ol girl had to feel that shit.

"Why the fuck yall doing this shit? Let me call my nigga and tell him to come get his ratchet ass bitch." That was all I needed to hear, and I punched his ass. Me and Halle were going to work. I'm sure Gino could have beaten my ass, but he knew that shit wouldn't play well with Spade. His ass was trying to bob and weave, but I was throwing them haymakers on behalf of La La.

All the times he hit her, fucked her face up, whatever the shit that was going on with her now. Every damn thing. I was beating this nigga like he did the shit to me. People tried their best to break it up, and then our ass was asked to leave. I knew Spade was more than likely going to put me in the basement for this stunt I pulled, so as I was leaving, I snatched Gino's steak off his plate.

"Bitch, did you really take his damn food? I can't with you right now. Give me a piece." Handing her some, I laughed as we tore that nigga shit up.

"Fuck yea I did. This shit good as fuck too. I'm mad as hell we had to leave. Bitch you know that nigga about to put me on punishment. It's good to know your ass can fight though. I wasn't sure since you always let me talk to you crazy."

"Bitch I'm not scared of you for real. The way you act out and the look you always have in your eyes, I just know you been through some shit and that's why you doing it. My ass be wanting to hug you, but your bitch ass might shoot me if I do. I've never met anyone who seems to have it all together, pretty as hell, and

pockets full of money but mean as hell. Your ass be wildin. Don't

get it twisted though, I can throw these hands."

"I see. I have been through some things, but it doesn't give

me the right to treat you like shit. For that, I'm sorry. Thank you

for putting up with my shit all this time. I'm going to miss living

with you bitch." We hugged, and the valet brought me my car.

"Damn that shit sexy." Irritated with his bullshit comment,

I threw my steak bone at his ass and it hit him in the eye.

"Come on bitch."

"See mean." Halle was looking at me in disbelief.

"I said sorry for being mean to you, not anybody else. Now

pray for me when I get home." I hoped Spade accepted my

apology just as easy. It was almost time for Tiana to be here. I

didn't want to be locked in the basement when we supposed to

be going out. Damn, I hoped I wasn't in trouble.

CHAPTER 22 TIANA

When Pebbles called me and told me I could come live with her, I was happy as fuck. My life was shit right now, but I would never let anyone know it. Not even Pebbles. Her shit was together, and I couldn't let her know that I had fallen off like bad dope. When she was here, both of us was on the top of our game. She had Bam, but I had niggas. I've always been able to make something out of nothing.

The first time I called her, my ass had just got put out and living in shelter. I was there three days and I knew the shit wasn't for me. Putting on my best clothes, I went out to the club in search for a sponsor. Something had to give, and I couldn't live that life. This nigga named Ju was in there throwing money around left and right and I knew he was my target. Boy, did I miss.

I landed the nigga, but it was nothing like it seemed. He begged me to move in after the first night and I thought I hit the jackpot. I pretended to play hard to get, but I was mentally packing the first time he suggested it. God was answering my

prayers, or so I thought. As soon as I moved in, I knew something

was wrong with the picture this nigga painted. His house didn't

match the money he was flaunting when I met him. His ass was

one door step away from being the shelter. That's how bad his

shit looked.

Having to know, I asked his ass what the fuck was really

going on. This nigga said the money he was in there flaunting was

his boss shit. Now that the nigga sobered up, he was panicking

because he had to pay the money back. If he didn't, his boss

would kill him and me because I was his girl. I looked at that nigga

like he lost his mind. As soon as he went to sleep, I was ghost up

out that bitch. My ass was telling my home girl what happened

when she started telling me all these stories about his boss. That

nigga was going to kill me, and I needed to go home and figure

out how me and Ju could fix this shit. I wasn't trying to die today.

When I got there, the first thing Ju told me was I needed to

start carrying my weight if I was going to live there. Looking around the house, I was lost on what he had to pay for living in a dump. After talking to him, his ass came up with a plan for me to sleep with a few of his homies for some bread. They were supposed to be paid and we could get the money fast and wouldn't owe his boss.

You know a bitch like me told him to fuck off. By the time he got through beating my ass, I was too scared not to. My first time, a bitch only got a hundred dollars. I asked Ju how much he owed his boss and the nigga told me one hundred thousand dollars. My pussy was going to fall off trying to pay off this debt. Since I been with him, that's all the fuck I did. Fuck his friends, get my ass beat, and cry myself to sleep.

Pebbles didn't know how bad I needed this escape. Most of them made me do things no human should ever have to do and some of them would beat my ass as well if I said no. After all that shit, I would go home only to find Ju laid on the couch drinking. That's all the fuck he did. His ass never did anything to try and get any money. His ass told me that was my payment for living off

LOCKED DOWN BY HOOD LOVE

him. I've tried to leave so many times, but his drunk ass would get off the couch then. I even went back to the shelter and the nigga beat my ass out the bed and all the way home. Nobody ever tried to help me and so many people have seen this nigga dog walking me.

I was so tired, I even tried to commit suicide. That nigga beat me until I threw the pills up. I've been pregnant by God knows who and a lot of other shit. Of course, he beat the baby out of my ass as well. I know this was not the life that was meant for me, but I had no idea how to get the fuck out with no help. That was the reason I finally reached out to my best friend. When she played me to the left, I knew I would die right where I was.

This had become my sad reality and I planned to blow my own brains out the night Pebbles called me. I couldn't believe how God stepped in and saved me right in that moment. I've been crying ever since and waiting on this nigga to pass out from drinking, so I could sneak out and be gone forever.

When I heard the bottle hit the floor, I made my move. Tip toeing, I headed to the front door. Even though he was drunk, I didn't want him to hear me and wake up. As soon as I got to the door, his ass grabbed me.

"Where the fuck you think you going?" Kneeing him in the dick, I took off running and never looked back. My ass didn't even stop for a cab until I was ten minutes away from the damn airport. My ass was crying and hyperventilating. It felt like I was about to die, but I was too scared to stop. That nigga has had a hold on me for years and I was over it. Now I knew what Pebbles meant when she said this chapter of her life was over and there was nothing left here for her. I could barely remember the good memories because of all the bad shit I went through.

Two hours later, I was safe on the plane and I knew Ju would never find me in Chicago. The nigga can't even afford a plane ticket, so I knew there was no way his ass would come looking for me. After all this time, I finally escaped, and I couldn't stop crying. The flight attendant kept walking past looking at me, trying to see why I was crying. She had no idea these were happy

tears and I didn't know how to explain it.

"Ma'am, are you okay? Are you scared to fly?"

"No, couldn't be better. I promise you I'm good. Happiest

day of my life." The lady smiled at me and walked off. I couldn't

wait for this plane to land. This was the first day of the rest of my

life. I was blessed to have a second chance, and I couldn't wait to

get started. Anything Pebbles needed me to do, I had her back.

She would never know how much I owed her for this shit.

As soon as I got off the plane, I ran to baggage claim. I

couldn't wait to breathe the Chicago air. That air represented

freedom and I wanted to choke on that shit. When I got my bags,

Pebbles and some fine ass nigga was standing there with a sign. It

had to be her nigga Spade, but her description didn't do him any

justice. This nigga was, bitch I'll make him biscuits from scratch

and suck the batter off his dick, fine.

"Best friend. I'm so glad you made it. I thought your ass

was going to change your mind. You know LA is your life. I almost didn't call you and ask you to come. Shit, I thought you were

joking." On the inside I was crying tears. If she thought I was

playing and never called me, I would still be back home going

through hell.

"When have you ever known me to play? Bitch they kicked

me off the basketball team because I wouldn't play. I'm in love

already."

"This is Jaleel, but everybody calls him Spade. I've been

looking for this nigga but didn't even know I was searching. He

found me, and I knew this was the person I was supposed to be

with. Spade this is my best friend Tiana." His fine ass standing

there just smiling like the happiest nigga on earth. She always did

land the good ones. Looking him over again, I looked at Pebbles

and she nodded as if she knew what I was thinking. I know one

thing, she lucky she found his fine ass first.

"Don't listen to shorty. She trying not to be on

punishment, that's the only reason her ass around here acting all

nice singing me praises and shit." We all laughed, and I couldn't believe he was admitting to that shit. The way she latched on and

kissed him, I knew his ass wasn't lying. Pebbled had done

something, and whatever it was, the shit was big.

"I'm sure you know her like I do, and punishment or not,

this bitch ain't gone ever change. Now, where your friends at. I

don't want to be staring at your ass all night and shit. You fine, but

this bitch likes to fight and I ain't trying to get put out and I just

got here."

"Calm down, I'll fill you in on everything including the

niggas. We gotta do it when Spade ain't around though. Let's get

you settled in. We gotta get dressed, we going out tonight." I was

ready for whatever.

CHAPTER 23 SPADE

These girls were crazy as hell, but I was glad to see Pebbles happy. This girl been here giving us hell, so if this was all she needed to make her feel better, then I was all for it. I'm sure she thought I was mad at her ass, but I wasn't. Gino called me as soon as she got put out the restaurant and told me what happened. His ass probably only did it because he thought she would tell me.

The nigga had been cleaning up his act, and it was the only reason his ass was still here. Him fucking a bitch I was running through don't mean shit to me, but I'm sure his ass was scared shitless. His ass knew he been on my bad side lately and any lil thing could cause him to get Spaded. Not no ran through ass bitch though. Driving to the warehouse, I was hoping the nigga was here. When I saw his car, I headed inside.

"Let me holla at you real quick." Gino came to the back office and sat down in my chair.

"What's up Spade?"

186

"Are we good now? I know you been all in your feelings over your bitch and that's why your ass was acting out. I fucked the bitch one time and didn't know she was your girl. Until the night at the club, I couldn't even tell you her name. You fucked a bitch I was smashing, so I ask you again. Are we good? We even now right? No more bullshit and no more disrespect. Your bitch ass got your lick back." I knew his ass wanted to lie about it, but it would be in his best interest to tell the truth. If he wanted to survive this meeting, I was going to need him to keep it real. If he lied to me, that meant I still couldn't trust his ass.

"Yeah we good now. It was never about you though. The only mother fucker I was pissed at was my bitch." I'm not sure if I believed him or not, but I nodded my head at his response. If I felt in any way his ass was starting to move different again, his time was up. There were no more chances for Gino and I hope he knew that shit. Grabbing a duffle bag, I placed a hundred keys inside from the safe. I was about to make a run, and I didn't have time to be going back and forth over a bitch I didn't want. If he wanted

Jontanae ass, he could have her. She was a good fuck, but a chick like her could never be my bitch.

"I'm glad you're here. This nigga approached me about some keys and they going for a cheaper rate. I had him checked out and he good. A lot of the homies are grabbing shit from him and I wanted to know what you thought about it."

"You know I don't do business with mother fuckers I don't know. Why his shit so cheap? How did he know to approach you? Where the fuck the nigga come from?" I had a million questions. A nigga in my position had to be on point.

"The nigga get his shit from Miami. His girl rides down every month and get the shit and bring it back. His ass trying to take over and figured he could do that by making his shit cheaper than anyone else's."

"Let me think on this shit and look into some stuff on my own. I'll get back to you on that. In the meantime, go get ready we going out tonight. My girl wants to show her best friend a good time and we are going to do just that. Leave your bullshit at

the door." Walking out with my bag of dope, I turned back to him.

"Oh and Gino, leave that bitch at home. If my girl has to

fight her one more time, I'm going to put a bullet in her head. My

bitch ain't about to be all ratchet out here in these streets over a

bitch that don't matter. You feel me?" He nodded his head, and I

walked out.

****

I know Pebbles just wanted to show off my house, she was

begging for me to let Tiana come over. I don't give a fuck how

gone I was off her ass, that's one thing I would never bend on. She

lucky her ass is here. My shorty was spoiled as shit in this little bit

of time, and her ass was in here pouting.

"Shvonne get dressed. You can continue to pout, and I'll

make your ass stay home. Don't make me shut this shit down. You

doing the most right now and you know what the fuck it is. If you

want to show out for your homie, go put on the shit I bought for

your ass today." The pout finally disappeared and now she

wanted to know what she had. You could see the anxious look on her face, and I had to try not to laugh.

"Jaleel don't play with me. Where is it?" Shaking my head, it was funny to me how easy she could switch emotions.

"In your closet and hurry up, I want your hair curly." I barely got to finish my sentence before she took off running. Following behind her, I walked upstairs to our bedroom. Shorty was admiring the Balenciaga dress and shoes I had gotten her. Giving me a kiss, she ran to jump in the shower. Chicks always took forever and that's why I get my shit out the way. I refuse to get ready after her ass. Pebbles took entirely too long for that shit.

Pulling out my Balenciaga button up and jeans, I threw my shit on. Deciding to rock my Red Bottoms, I threw my jewelry on and I was ready to go. An hour later, I was still waiting on Pebbles to come out of the fucking shower. This shit didn't make no sense. Right when I was about to tell her we were staying home, she walked out. Head full of curls looking sexy as fuck. The water running off her body had my dick hard and I knew we weren't

about to make it to the club any time soon.

"Hey, bring your pretty ass over here and suck my dick.

You been watching the videos I showed you right?" My shorty was

good, but I needed her to be great. If I could eat her pussy like it

was the last supper, then she could suck my dick like a popsicle on

a hot summer day.

"You not ready for this shit. I been practicing." Giving her a

deadly look, she knew what I assumed she meant. "Not on

another nigga, on Feelo." I hated that damn toy, but if it made her

better, then I was all for it.

"Come show me." Crawling to me, I had to hold back my

excitement. My bitch was fine enough to make a nigga cum from

looking at her. Pulling my dick out, I couldn't wait to feel her lips

on my shit. The first thing she did was spit on it, and I knew this

shit was about to be fye as fuck.

Not even playing around, she deep throated my dick.

Trying not to sound like a bitch, I did everything I could to keep

191

my moans down. Grabbing her by her hair, I damn near pulled

that shit off her scalp trying not to sound like a bitch. My shorty

didn't even stop. Pebbles was sucking that mother fucker like her

freedom depended on it. You could tell she was into that shit, cus

she was moaning and talking shit.

"I bet I don't need to watch shit else, do I? Who the fuck

own this dick?" I couldn't even answer because I was trying not to

cum quick, but that shit was looking inevitable. "Talk shit now

nigga." My ass could barely move my lips, let alone respond to her

ass. Not being able to hold it any longer, I came in her mouth. I

waited for her ass to spit the shit out, but my shorty swallowed

that shit like a G. There was no way I would ever let her go. Fuck

what my mama was talking about, I needed her in my life.

CHAPTER 24 GINO

Looking over to my right, I couldn't believe I was laying

here in bed with Tiana. I knew from the jump that I wanted her

ass, but I just knew it was no way in hell Pebbles would let that

shit fly. Sitting here smiling, I thought about last night.

When Spade and them walked in the club, I was already in

VIP drinking. I wanted to be chill to make sure I didn't have any

kind of incidents. Last time we were here, I allowed my emotions

to get the best of me. Not tonight though. I needed Spade to do

this deal and if I acted the fuck out, there was no way he would.

Looking over the club, I saw them before they saw me. You

could tell baby girl didn't have money like Pebbles did, but she

was fine as hell and I knew she had potential. Spade lucked up

and got his, but I didn't mind getting the next best thing. Halle

was cute as well, but she wouldn't give me none off the strength

of La La. Thinking about her pissed me off. If the bitch had kept her mouth shut about our relationship, I could fuck any of these hoes.

Spade gave me that nigga be cool look and I laughed. I guess he could see the look in my eye and knew what the fuck I was on. The girls must have been drinking before they got here or something, they came in the section turned up. I've never seen Pebbles like this, but she was going crazy. They twerked damn near to every song that came on. It was a damn good view, but I was pissed I couldn't fuck shit. At least that's what I thought.

Beyoncé came on and the girls got on some other shit. Pebbles straddled Spade, Halle got on Bruno, and Tiana climbed on me. When she got to grinding, I wanted to slide my dick out and fuck her right there in the club. After the song went off, Tiana didn't bother to get up. Not wanting to think too much into it, I just chilled and went off her vibe.

Crazy as it may seem, we all had a great time. We stayed until the lights came on and everybody was feeling good. Halle didn't even say bye, nor did she give a fuck about who was driving

194

with who. Baby girl stumbled her ass past us holding Bruno hand

and was out. That nigga girl was going to kill him. She may be just

as crazy as Pebbles. Not wanting to get my hopes up, dapped up

Spade and got ready to head out. I'm not into making an ass out

of myself, so I was not trying to make a move.

"Hey Gino, you think you can take me home? Halle just left

my ass like I wasn't shit. If it's not too much to ask." Not wanting

to start no shit, I looked over at Spade and Pebbles. Both of them

shrugged and my dick damn near jumped out of my pants.

"I got you. Let's go." As soon as we got in the car, she was

all over my ass. I'm not sure if it was the liquor or if she just

wanted a nigga. Either way I was happy as fuck.

"Let's just go back to your place." That's what the fuck I

did. We went about three rounds. I'm glad my pull out game was

strong because I didn't use not one condom. My ass was tired as

fuck this morning, but I needed to get up and go handle some

business. Sliding out of my bed, I tried my best not to wake her.

When I got back, I wanted some more of that pussy.

Walking in the bathroom I handled my hygiene and got dressed. I needed Spade to do this deal and I was going to make it happen. Heading to see Peemo, went to the warehouse they worked out of. Parking my car, I got out and went inside.

"What up nigga. I talked to Spade, but he not really feeling this meeting and shit. I need you to make him feel it. Let me get one of your bricks so he could try it out. If he thinks the shit is good, he gone come holla at you."

"You telling me to give you a free brick just to get a nigga to come and talk to me? What kind of shit is that bruh?"

"The kind of shit that's going to get you what you want. The nigga needs an incentive and I'm trying to give him one. Otherwise, the shit dead. It's up to you." Grabbing a brick off his desk, he threw it to me.

"He better take this meeting or you owe me for this brick and my time."

"I got you." Placing the shit under the hood of my car, I drove back to our warehouse to convince Spade to do this

196

meeting. I'm trying to better my future and this was the only way I knew how to do that. This shit was going to be the lick that put me on and I needed Spade as to get on board. Pulling up to our warehouse, I got the key out of the hood and walked inside. Seeing his Maserati outside, I knew he was here.

"Yooo I got something I want you to try out." Handing him the dope, you could see he was aggravated with me.

"I thought we talked about this already. I'm not on that with some niggas I don't know. I'm straight on that shit." I knew he was going to say that.

"Just try it and if it's bad, fuck it. No harm no foul." Rubbing his hand down his face, he grabbed his knife out of his pocket and cut the plastic. Placing it on his tongue, the nigga eye's bucked.

"This shit is pure and it's stronger than any shit we done ever had. Who the fuck is this nigga again?" Smiling, I knew I had him.

"His name Peemo. He gets the shit from Miami. All he wants is fourteen, you can't beat that shit."

"Arrange the meeting. I'll go meet up with his ass tomorrow. You know I don't make deals without a sit down. If shit sound good to me, it's a go. Tell that nigga he ain't getting this brick back either. Nigga gotta pay me for my time." We both laughed as he threw the brick in the safe. We both headed out, I'm sure he was going home to his bitch. I was heading back to Peemo to set this shit up.

Just the thought of it had me doing the Stevie J hand rub. This was big, and I couldn't wait for it go down. A nigga was about to be set for life. I was going to celebrate by going home to fuck that good ass pussy laying in my bed.

CHAPTER 25 SHVONNE

Rolling over, I played in Spade's dreads. He really was fine as fuck. I couldn't believe I was laying here next to him, but it was time I stopped crying over Bam. I needed to be strong and be the bitch he knew I was. His eyes opened, and he smiled at me. His grill was shining early, and he hadn't even brushed yet. When he looked at me, you could see a sparkle in his eyes. I wish I could look at him with that same glare, but I was damaged. Too much had happened to me.

"Shorty why you up looking at me on that creep shit. You know bitches that stare at their nigga while their sleeping will kill their ass? Females think they got one up on us, but I watch snapped too."

"Shut your dumb ass up and if you call me another bitch, you won't have to be sleep for me to kill you. Where are you going? I know you're tired because you have never stayed sleep this late."

"That pussy put me in a coma. I got a meeting today and then I'm going to go meet up with Gino at his spot right after. If this meeting goes well, I'm leaving this drug shit where it's at in a year. A nigga tired of running the streets. I don't want to be like my father old as fuck and in the streets. My ass wants kids and shit. Hell, I could walk away now if I wanted too, but I have to make sure everything is good and in place."

"Who the fuck giving you kids? I don't want babies, so get that shit out of your head." It took everything in me to try and make it sound normal, but the thought of me getting pregnant again and losing it was killing me.

"You saying that shit now, but I been pretending to pull out. A nigga be done already nutted in you and let some of it out on your ass. Niggas trap bitches too. Your ass gone be tied to me for life whether you want to or not." He walked over to the safe in our room and put the code in. The bitch was big as hell, from the floor to the ceiling. Even though I didn't want him to know it, a bitch was watching closely. It was always good to know where the money was. You never know. Pulling out twenty stacks, he

handed it to me.

"I'm sure Tiana needs clothes and shit, so yall can go

shopping today while I go handle my business. That dress she had

on last night was falling the fuck apart. You know I can't have that

shit. My name on the line." My ass tried not to laugh, but he

wasn't lying at all. I pulled like three strings from the bitch. I

already had plans, but I don't mind shopping. A girl can always

shop.

"Thank you baby. I was thinking that maybe you can put

me on your team. I'm just here doing nothing, but I'm a valuable

asset to have."

"You can get that shit out of your head. You don't ever

have to do shit. What's mine is yours. I'm your nigga and I got

you. I'd be fucked up if something happened to you behind my

shit." Not responding, I got up and started looking for something

to wear.

"I hear you, but just know a bitch like me can run through some money. Do you see the kind of clothes I wear? My running shoes cost fourteen hundred dollars." He just laughed.

"You must think I'm some poot boot ass nigga. Before I ever touched a baggie, I was a millionaire. My father died and left us five hundred million. I was fifteen then. Trust me, I got more money than I can count. We good. Hey, I got something for you." Walking over to closet, he pulled out a box. My ass got excited, he knew I loved surprises. When I opened it, there was a chain made up of all diamonds with a diamond spade hanging from it. Grabbing it from the box, he put it around my neck.

"When niggas see you out in the street, I want them to know you're King Spades girl. Don't ever take that shit off." The shit was beautiful. I don't know how many diamonds was in this thing, but it was sparkling like a mother fucker. Tears started to form, but I refused to do this. He was trying to tear down my walls and I didn't like it. Spade wanted to erase Bam from my heart, but I couldn't allow that shit. Bam was all I knew, and I had to carry on

202

LOCKED DOWN BY HOOD LOVE

his memory. He was my everything and I didn't know how to love him and move on. I couldn't. What I lost, no man could ever give that back to me.

"Thank you. I absolutely love it and I promise to always wear it. This will always remind me of you and what you were to me."

"Hold on bitch you speaking in past tense and shit. Don't be trying to kill me off and shit. I know you lost someone, but I'm not going nowhere." Slapping him in the head, I walked off to get in the shower. I didn't mean to speak past tense. Laughing at his expression from my choice of words, I proceeded to fix my hygiene.

When I got out of the shower, Spade was already gone. I needed to hurry my ass up because Tiana had called me before Spade woke up. She was at Gino's house waiting on me. His ass left her there and it wasn't any food in the house. She was going to kill me for taking this long to come pick her up. I told her over an hour ago that I was on the way. Throwing on an all black

Chanel jogging suit, I slid on my black Huaraches and headed out.

Looking in my phone at the address she gave me, I drove towards

her house. Spade was shocked that I didn't try to stop Tiana from

going with Gino. I told his ass she was grown, and he was the one

trying to convince me that La La was okay. Besides, I told her all

about that situation and she made her choice.

Was I okay with it, fuck yeah. Every person has the right to

choose what they want to do in life. She was my best friend and I

had her back to the fullest. When I pulled up to the house, I

laughed at how cheap this nigga was. If him and Spade were best

friends since he was kids, he had to have at least half of the

money Spade had. You wouldn't tell by the house his ass was

living in.

Nothing special stood out about this house at all. Hell, I

could buy a house better than this shit. Getting out my car, I

knocked on the door and waited for her to answer. She came to

the door with an attitude.

"It took your bitch ass long enough. I know it did not take that long for you to get here from your house. Come on, I told Gino I would meet him at the warehouse to get some money. He not coming home for another hour and I thought your ass would be here by now."

"Stop complaining, it's a beautiful day outside and it's about to get better. After we finish what we have to do, Spade gave me some money for us to go shopping."

"I sholl appreciate it. That chain nice as fuck." Reaching my hand up to my neck, a lot of thoughts flooded my mind. This nigga loved me, but I didn't think I could love him back. Ever. Bam would always have my heart.

CHAPTER 26 SPADE

Leaving the house, I almost wanted to turn around and go back. It was something in her eyes that wasn't right, and I could tell she went to her dark place again. I don't know what I have to do to help heal her and stop her from thinking about that nigga. My ass be trying to be understanding, but that shit not working. I was a selfish nigga, but I don't think it's a nigga out here walking the streets wanting their girl crying over the next nigga.

Money could never buy happiness, but I was also giving her something I've never given to any bitch. Me. Pebbles had my heart, but it was like she didn't want that shit. How could you force someone to love you, when they were determined to keep loving a nigga that was dead? It's like I was competing with a damn ghost and I wasn't cut out for that kind of shit.

After I was done with this meeting and hollering at Gino, me and Pebbles was going to have a serious talk. If she wasn't going to fully try, I was gone have to give up. This was unfamiliar territory for me, and I didn't know how to deal with it. My shorty

was breaking me down and her ass didn't realize it, or she didn't

give a fuck. From the first time I laid eyes on her, I knew I had to

have her. Everything about her told me she was different. Maybe

that wasn't a good thing and she was too damaged to accept love.

Her entire personality was based off her losing someone

and putting her guard up. If she got over him, will she be the same

person? It was too much on my mind before I went to this

meeting and maybe that meant I needed to turn around. Before I

could second guess myself, I realized I was there. May as well get

the shit over with.

It was only supposed to be me and Peemo, so I didn't have

to go through a security check. Walking until I saw him, I sat down

in the chair that was open. The nigga just stared at me and I got

an uneasy feeling.

"I finally get to meet the infamous King Spade. I'm Peemo

thanks for sitting down with me." Nodding my head at him, I

wanted him to lead the conversation. I wasn't about to let the next nigga feel like I needed them. My ass acted as if I was here doing him a favor.

"As you know Gino arranged this meeting under the pretense of you buying bricks from me at a lower price. You know damn well ain't nobody selling that shit that low. I'm sure you're wondering the real reason I brought you here." The nigga paused for dramatic affect. "Me and a few of my associates feel it's time for you to step down. You had a nice run and your ass should be paid out the ass by now. It's my time and I'm giving you the chance to bow out gracefully." I couldn't wait to get out of here, Gino ass was all out of chances. His ass would be dead as soon as I get the fuck up out of this jam.

"Maybe Gino should have told you who the fuck I am nigga. I don't bow to even tie my shoes I pay a bitch to do that. If you want something from me, your bitch ass gone have to come take it. The question is, can you take it."

"Nigga do you..." That was all he got out before I put a bullet in his head. As I said before, my father taught me a valuable lesson. If a nigga even looked like he was gone try to take me out, I got his ass first. No questions asked I would never be King Leel, I was better than that nigga. Hearing a shot let off, my ass ducked behind the desk to try and see where it was coming from. Obviously, this nigga wasn't alone.

Seeing the nigga try to creep up behind the chair, I shot him in his legs then gave his ass a chest shot as he fell to the ground. Three more men appeared, and I had to take them out strategically as well. Once I was sure I was the only left standing, I came out from behind the desk. Feeling around in my pocket, I was pissed I didn't have my knife. Taking my gun, I shot they ass a few more times just to make myself happy.

Leaving out, I felt incomplete. There wasn't a nigga I killed I didn't leave my spade on his shit. I had a good mind to go find a knife or even go by one and come back to finish the job. As bad as I wanted to leave my mark, it was someone else I wanted to kill more. Gino ass had to go, and I wasn't giving him another second to breathe my air. I'm glad it wasn't any police out or I would have gotten pulled over for sure. My ass was pushing this bitch trying

to get there. When I pulled up, I was glad I didn't have to wait.

The nigga's car was outside, so I knew he was here. All I could do

was pray Tiana wasn't over here with him, because I didn't leave

witnesses. I didn't know that bitch and I wasn't sure if she would

snitch. Her and Pebbles were best friends, but my shorty was a

ridah. You could tell it was in her DNA.

Not even bothering to knock, gun drawn I kicked the door

in. Funny thing is, the nigga only gave me his address to meet him

here after because he thought my ass wasn't going to make it out.

The house was dark, and I was alert trying to make sure this nigga

didn't run up on me. When my feet started sticking to the floor, I

tried to back out and tripped over something. Searching for the

light, I turned them on and Gino was laying there dead as a

mother fucker and I bugged out.

Not because the nigga was dead, I was happy for that shit.

His ass needed to be tortured. What was fucking me up was the

spade that was carved in his face and my knife lying next to his body. Somebody was trying to frame me for Gino's murder.

Grabbing my knife, I was about to get the fuck out of there. As I

walked out the door, I pulled my phone out to call Bruno. I

needed a clean up crew over here fast as fuck.

"Freeze. Put your hands where I can see them. Don't

move. Put your hands on your head and get on the ground." This

shit could not be happening. How the fuck did I get caught for a

murder I didn't commit, and I been killing niggas for years.

"You have the right to remain silent. Anything you say can

and will be used against you in a court of law. You have the right

to an attorney. If you can't afford an attorney, one would be

appointed for you." Out of all my years in these streets, I have

never seen the back of a police car. Pissed wasn't the word. Bruno

or someone from the crew had to set me up. Nobody else had

access to my office.

I needed to figure out which one of them niggas, and

Pebbles say she is useful, I was going to need her to get that info

out of there ass. At any means necessary. She talks a good talk, now it was time to see if my shorty was really about that life.

Unless I could get the judge to give me a bond. All I needed to do

was get out of this bitch, I would make these niggas talk. Thinking

about it, I had never been to jail before. I'm sure I could get out

on a bond. I would have to give Pebbles my code, but desperate

times called for desperate measures.

It was game time and these niggas fucked with the wrong

one. Crazy thing is, I was nothing like my father. Everybody ate

and got paid well. Anybody wanting to take me out, had to just be

a greedy mother fucker. That greed was about to be their

downfall though. All I needed was a phone call.

CHAPTER 27 SHVONNE

"Are you really about to buy that damn dress? That mother fucker is seven hundred dollars. Your man must be ugly paid." Laughing at Tiana cheap ass, I placed my dress on the counter.

"Why do you care how much it costs? Spade gave it to us to spend. Me and you, so bitch you better grab some shit or your ass gone come up short."

"Fuck that, just give me my ten stacks. I could use that shit for something else." Getting aggravated, I had to let her know she was in a different league. Before I could respond, my phone rung.

"Hello."

"Shvonne, it's me shorty. I'm in jail. Somebody killed Gino and they framed me for it."

"What the fuck? Baby where are you? What are they saying? Fuck." My ass was going crazy.

"Bitch what happened?"

213

"Somebody killed Gino." I whispered to Tiana.

"Shorty calm down and don't panic. I need you to step up and be my ridah. First, I need you to call my attorney. Take his number down." Typing it in my notes, I made sure I had it right.

"I got it baby, do you need me to come bond you out?"

"Shorty, I don't have a bond yet. I go tomorrow, and I need you to be there. Whatever they say it is, go home and get it so you can pay it. I'll give you the pass code. If they don't give me a bond, I'm going to need you to be me and find out who the fuck is behind this."

"Jaleel don't say that. You are going to get a bond. I don't know if I can be you baby. How the fuck did this happen." My ass had gotten loud and drew attention of the people standing by.

"Straighten the fuck up. You are not a weak bitch and I don't have time to pacify you right now. You're King Spade's shorty. Act like it. You got your chain on?"

"Yes, I told you I will never take it off."

"Then you're good. They will respect you and give you info off that alone. If you're anything like the person you been portraying, you got this shit. Now repeat after me and say I'm in charge." Hearing him pretend he was Djay from Hustle and Flow brought a smile to my face and made me laugh.

"I'm in charge."

"Okay, you got this shorty. I'll see you at the county tomorrow at 9. Pebbles, I know I never said it before, but I love you." He must have known I wouldn't say it back, because he hung up. I was so not ready for that shit. Paying for my stuff, we walked out of the store. Walking to the car, we got in and I called his lawyer. After explaining everything, I agreed to meet up with him to pay his fee. Before I could pull off, Tiana ass stopped me dead in my tracks.

"If Gino wouldn't have been killed, he would have died anyway." Looking at her like she was crazy, I had no idea what the fuck she was talking about. My ass needed to get to the lawyer and give him this money, so I can make sure his ass was at court tomorrow. Her ass wants to talk in riddles and shit, but the look on her face kept me intrigued.

"What the fuck you talking about best friend? You know you always did that shit. Anytime something bad happened, you didn't like dealing with it and changed the subject. It was like. You thought you could make it go away if you talked about something else." When I laughed, I expected her to as well, but she didn't.

"I have HIV. When we had sex, we didn't use a condom. If he hadn't been killed, he would have died slow." This was why we as a people needed to be educated. She didn't look sick at all and I never would have thought something was wrong with her.

"Best friend how? You don't look like you have anything. I'm so sorry, I don't even know what to say."

"The nigga I was messing with was pimping my ass out to pay for his debt. I been through so much since you left me friend. Why did you leave me behind to go through that? They hurt me bad and I needed you. I was back home suffering and you were out here living the life." Hugging her, I didn't know what to say. I never thought about it that way and now I felt like shit. She had

my ass crying and this was the first time I cried about something

other than Bam.

"I'm so sorry best friend. I didn't know. If you would have

told me, I would have come to rescue your ass. I love you so much

and we are going to get through this." Thinking of something, I

asked something I had to know.

"If you knew you had it, why did you let him fuck you

without a condom?" She actually started laughing.

"You told me about that shit with La La and you hadn't

said anything about a plan, so I figured let me show you I was

good for something. That nigga was gone think about that shit the

rest of his life." We both fell out laughing.

"Come on girl, let me go pay this damn lawyer before

Spade curse my ass out." Heading to the lawyer's office, I thought

about what Tiana confessed. That was some heavy shit, but how

did she expect me to save her, if she never told me what she was

going through. Her ass would ask to come with me, but she would always act as if her life was going good. I made a mental note to make it my business to pay her ex nigga a visit. Even though he was dying slow, I felt the need to speed that shit up.

****

"The people versus Jaleel Spade." His lawyer stood up and walked to the front. I sat in court and watched Spade walk out looking as fine as he was yesterday. There wasn't any worry written on his face or in his eyes. That cocky shit was a turn on. He stood before the judge licking his lips and them golds were shining.

I listened to the State's Attorney run down his charges. The lawyer already told me they found him leaving the scene with the murder weapon on him. They also had his gun that tied him to some other murders from the same night. It wasn't looking good, but he was a cocky lawyer and felt he could get him off. I drifted off thinking about the day before when I heard the judge yell out.

"No bail." Spade turned to me and it looked like he didn't have a care in the world. My ass stared on in shock, but his lawyer was trying to convince him it was okay, and he would get right on his defense.

"Shvonne, you're me now. You got this. Do what I need you to do and you get me out of here."

"I got you Jaleel." Just to piss the judge off I started screaming in the courtroom. "Free King Spade. Free King Spade." The bailiff came and dragged my ass the fuck up out of there. I didn't give a fuck, I screamed that shit all the way to my car.

Putting my shades on, I drove the fuck off in my Bugatti. The first thing I did was head to his warehouse. This was the start of something special. They had unleashed a monster.

Walking into the warehouse, you would have thought I owned that bitch. Mother fuckers were sitting around, and I wasn't about to have that shit. I needed to make sure they understood that they weren't dealing with your everyday chick. Walking up to a guy I didn't know, but he had to be in the crew. His ass was too fucking comfortable. Mother fucker was drinking and cracking jokes. It's as if they didn't have any fucks to give, but they were about to have some after this meeting. It was time to

meet Queen P. Pulling my gun out, I shot him in the head with no

questions.

"I'm now in charge of the organization in Spade's absence.

If I think you trying to play me because I'm a bitch, you will end up

just like this nigga."

"Where is Spade and why the fuck you think you're in

charge? It's levels to this shit." I liked Bruno, but he better check

his tone fast.

"Spade is in jail for killing Gino. Until we find out who the

fuck set him up, he put me in charge. The way you popping off

make me feel like I need to be checking into you. While he is

away, I am over anything King Spade. Are we clear? Or do we

have a problem?"

"If he put you in charge, then we have your back. Just tell

us what it is we need to do. If somebody set my nigga up, we gone

figure that shit out." Nodding my head, it was time to get down to

business. These niggas looked at me with fear in their hearts, and that's exactly how I wanted them. Rubbing the chain around my neck, I whispered to myself. I'm in charge. Knowing I made my point, I walked off to my office. The sound of my Giueseppes was the only thing you could hear as I walked away.

Grabbing my phone, I called my right hand man. Tiana picked up on the first ring. You could tell she wasn't sure about revealing her secret to me. What she didn't know was that deadly weapon was going to come in handy.

"You ready to put in work bitch."

"I'm on the way."

CHAPTER 28 SPADE

Sitting in my cell, I couldn't believe my ass was in this shit hole. I've been going over the shit in my mind trying to figure out what the fuck I missed. It had to be Bruno's ass, and I was kicking myself for missing all the signs. That was my lil nigga and I saved Gino from killing him on numerous occasions. This entire time, I thought it was Gino on some snake shit, but it was the lil nigga I raised and groomed from the start.

I've been waiting to hear from Shvonne with some good news that she got a mother fucker to confess, but that shit has yet to happen. It's been six months and we still don't know which one of these niggas set me up. I needed her to torture Bruno and try to get the info out of him. It had to be his ass, that was the only thought I kept coming back to.

This shit was starting to take a toll on me, but it was hitting my mama more. She was looking a fucking mess and every time she came; her ass broke down and left screaming and crying. It

222

got so bad I had to tell her to stay at home. I couldn't stand breaking my moms heart and I was strong enough to do this shit without her having to be here. Shvonne was the ridah I knew she was. My shorty handled all my business and it was good to know I picked the right bitch to be by my side.

"Spade you got a visitor." Knowing it was my shorty, a smile came over my face and for the first time today, my ass was in a good mood. The guard escorted me to the visiting cage and she was sitting there looking like new money. I never had to give her the pass code to my safe because I had too much money coming in. She would be set for the rest of her life just off the work she was putting in. If she ever needed it, I would give to her ass in a heartbeat. The money I got from my father is hidden away. I would never put all my money in one spot and I was glad I did that shit.

"Hey baby. You still looking fine as ever. You better not be somebody's bitch in here. You know I got my ears to the streets and these niggas will come out talking." If she was anybody else, I would have cursed her ass the fuck out for saying some shit like

that, but I knew it was her trying to make me smile.

"Get the fuck out of here. You know I go for sentencing

tomorrow. It's now or never shorty. I need you to put some

pressure on a mother fucker. I'm thinking you need to focus on

Bruno. You got to get a nigga to talk or this shit is over for me."

You could see the sadness come in her eyes, but she tried not to

let it show.

"Your lawyer told me it would be a lost cause. If that was

the only thing they had you on, we could work with that. The gun

that did the other murders, and the countless bodies they found

with the spade on their face is not helping you. I'm so sorry I

failed you baby, I really tried to be you." Seeing her cry broke my

heart. None of this was on her. It was my dumb ass that thought

the shit would be cool if I left my signature on every nigga I killed.

It was my ass that got caught with a gun that had bodies on it. My

prints were at the scene of the other murder. All that shit fell on

me. I hated that she probably sat around blaming herself. I never should have put that kind of pressure on her to make her think my

freedom depended on her.

"Look shorty, this shit falls on me. I got too fucking cocky.

All I need you to do is stay strong for a nigga. I would never ask

you to wait on me, but don't forget about me. Keep my books

laced and answer the phone when I call. Is that too much to ask of

you?" Shvonne ass started doing the ugly cry and I wish I could

hold her. You have enough money to last you a life time, but if

you need more I got you. Tell Bruno the business is his. Go live

your life shorty."

"I'll come visit every weekend and we don't know how

long you are going to get. You can't expect me to just walk away

from you. I'll hand everything over to Bruno, but I will not walk

away from you." Just knowing she wanted to ride it out with me

had a nigga feeling good, but I couldn't ask her to do that shit for

me.

"I'll see you tomorrow. Make sure your ass looking good for a nigga. You know you out there representing me and I don't want niggas thinking I had a raggedy bitch."

"You lucky I can't slap your ass. I'll see you tomorrow and I'll pray for you baby." Blowing her a kiss, I got up and walked back to my room. I knew that Bruno confessing wouldn't have gotten me off, but Gino's murder is the one that's getting me connected to the others. The shit at the warehouse could be argued self defense, but none of that mattered without a confession. My fate was in the judge's hands, I just hoped he had mercy on my ass.

****

Shvonne was sitting front row looking good as fuck, smiling at her, I took my seat. The judge walked in and I tried my best to stay looking strong and confident for my shorty, but the shit was hard. My life was in this nigga's hands and I had no idea what he was going to do.

"Jaleel Spade. You are a threat to society and I feel that I would be putting the lives of many in danger if I allow you to walk these streets again. With me knowing the type of pain you have inflicted on thousands of families leads me to believe that you are a terrorist. Therefore, I will sentence you as such. I hereby sentence you to three hundred and twenty five years in prison without the possibility of parole." I never understood why they gave niggas numbers like that when it wasn't a soul living that long. His bitch ass could have just said life without parole.

All the other shit was just extra. When I heard my shorty scream, it took my mind off of the judge. Turning around to face her, the shit broke my heart. Her body was shaking uncontrollably, and the tears were flowing like a river. Not caring since a nigga wasn't getting out anyway, I reached over the bench and hugged her.

"It's going to be okay shorty. I did this shit to myself. You got enough money to get the fuck out of here. Go live your life. I love you and I'm grateful to have met you." Kissing her, the bailiff started dragging me away. That only made her cry harder. Shit

was breaking a nigga.

"I love you shorty, don't you ever forget that."

"I love you to Spade. I'm sorry I never told you, but I love

you." When she said that shit, I couldn't stop the tears that fell

from my eyes. I could go away knowing I did what I set out to do, I

healed her. Now I had to live the rest of my life knowing I broke

her again.

****

ONE YEAR LATER...

I've been in Statesville Correctional Facility for a year now

and I was just getting to the point where I could go to sleep and

not dream about Shvonne. Shorty had me and I couldn't believe I

fucked that shit up. Every night, I thought about different shit I

could have done to avoid me being here. If I had killed Gino when

he first started acting flaw, I never would have taken that meeting

and went to kill him after. It was so many mistakes I made and wish I had done shit another way. At the end of the day, all I was doing was torturing myself. The shit was done, and I would die in here. After seeing the toll this shit was taking on Shvonne, I took her off my visitors list and I would only call.

Since I stopped our visits, she sounded like she was doing a lot better. Every time I would call, she would be somewhere else in the world. I wish I could be out there with her enjoying the money I worked so hard for. Instead, the shit was just collecting dust. I've been thinking it over for a while, and I was going to tell her tonight where the rest of the money was with all my pass codes. There was more than enough money on my books and I barely used it. Mother fuckers gave me everything just because I was King Spade.

"Spade nurse visit." I'm glad the finally called me down for it because I had a tooth ache out of this world. When I was heading down the hall, I saw Bruno. If he was in here who the fuck was running the business?

"Nigga what the fuck you doing in here? I know you're not stupid enough to get caught with nothing? If you're here, who the fuck running my shit?" He lucky I even gave it to him since I wasn't sure if he set me up or not.

"Nigga what the fuck are you talking about? The mother fucker you left in charge is running it. Queen P got shit on lock out there." My ass was lost as to who the fuck that was.

"Nigga who the fuck is Queen P?" Now he was looking at me crazy.

"Pebbles nigga. She said you put her in charge and we all been working for her."

"I did put her in charge in the beginning. When I got sentenced, I told her to hand everything over to you."

"She ain't said shit like that to me."

"Spade, let's go." Hurrying my ass to the nurse, I needed to get back to the tier, so I could call her ass. This girl got a taste of the streets and now she was addicted to the shit. My ass done created a monster. With me being in here, I couldn't stop her. If that was the life she wanted to live, then I would let her. She probably feels like it has her closer to me. I wouldn't take that from her, but I was going to curse her ass out about lying to me. If she wanted to stay in charge, I would have let her.

When I got back to the tier, I called her phone, but the number was disconnected. Calling my moms, I had her try to do a three way. I got the same result.

"Ma, go by my house. Something might be wrong. I know you don't like her, but this is not like Shvonne. We talk damn near every day. If somebody set me up, they may have went after her. I'll call you back in an hour."

"Nigga you lucky I love your ass. This Salt Lake butter looking bitch better not give me no attitude either. Your ass chasing her when you got all that boy pussy in there with you."

"Bye ma. I'll call you in an hour." It seemed like time was going by slow as fuck and I was going crazy watching the clock. If something happened to her, I would lose my fucking mind. My ass was pacing the floor and I damn near broke my finger dialing my moms when the hour was up. She answered on the first ring and my heart sank. Someone had done something to my baby. Fuck.

"Son, she cleaned you out. It is nothing in this mother fucker and your safe is wide open and not a rubber band is in that bitch. I told you it was something about her ass, but you didn't want to listen."

"Ma, go to the garage." When she walked in, I could tell my shit was gone. The echo was too damn loud.

"That shit gone too. It is one car in here though. An old ass white Benz with California plates." Hanging up the phone, my heart was racing trying to figure out why Shvonne robbed me. Out of nowhere everything started to hit me at once.

She robbed me when no one in the world was bold enough to do that shit. The first day I met her she was focused on my tattoo. When we were in the car talking, she asked me why did I just up and kill people. Why didn't I need a reason? Every time I turned around, she was crying over her ex that was killed. When I got shot at, I was leaving Shvonne's house. Her best friend leaving with Gino even though she knew what he did to La La and she didn't say a word. Before I left out, I told her I had that meeting and then I was going to Gino's house. In court one of the murders they charged me with was from some guy in California I killed at the club. Shvonne was from California. Her leaving the Benz in my garage was her letting me know.

My ass was standing in the day room having flash back after flash back. Once the shit started running back to me, I knew exactly what the fuck happened. THIS BITCH SET ME UP.

"The court awaited as the foreman got the verdict from the bailiff. Emotional outbursts tears and smeared makeup. He stated, he was guilty on all charges. She's shaking looking like she took it the hardest. A spin artist, she brought her face up laughing. That's when the prosecutor realized what happened. All that speaking her mind testifying and crying when this bitch did the crime. The Queenpin. Before you lock my love away." Testify- Common

To Be Continued...

KEEP UP WITH LATOYA NICOLE

Like my author page on fb @misslatoyanicole

My fb page Latoya Nicole Williams

IG Latoyanicole35

Twitter Latoyanicole35

Snap Chat iamTOYS

Reading group: Toy's House of Books

Email latoyanicole@yahoo.com

OTHER BOOKS BY LATOYA NICOLE

NO WAY OUT: MEMOIRS OF A HUSTLA'S GIRL

NO WAY OUT 2: RETURN OF A SAVAGE

GANGSTA'S PARADISE

GANGSTA'S PARADISE 2: HOW DEEP IS YOUR LOVE

ADDICTED TO HIS PAIN (STANDALONE)

LOVE AND WAR: A HOOVER GANG AFFAIR

LOVE AND WAR 2: A HOOVER GANG AFFAIR

LOVE AND WAR 3: A HOOVER GANG AFFAIR

LOVE AND WAR 4: A GANGSTA'S LAST RIDE

CREEPING WITH THE ENEMY: A SAVAGE STOLE MY HEART

1-2

I GOTTA BE THE ONE YOU LOVE (STANDALONE)

THE RISE AND FALL OF A CRIME GOD: PHANTOM AND

ZARIA'S STORY

THE RISE AND FALL OF A CRIME GOD 2: PHANTOM AND

ZARIA'S STORY

ON THE 12TH DAY OF CHRISTMAS MY SAVAGE GAVE TO ME

A CRAZY KIND OF LOVE: PHANTOM AND ZARIA

14 REASONS TO LOVE YOU: A LATOYA NICOLE ANTHOLOGY

SHADOW OF A GANGSTA

THAT GUTTA LOVE 1-2

?

BOOK 21, AND I CAN'T BELIEVE IT. FIVE NUMBER ONES, I'M STILL IN DISBELIEF. YOU GUYS ARE AWESOME, AND I LOVE YOU. THANK YOU FOR CONTINOUSLY MAKING MY BOOKS A SUCCESS. WITHOUT YOU THERE IS NO ME. MAKE SURE YOU DOWNLOAD, SHARE, READ AND REVIEW. MORE BOOKS WILL BE COMING FROM ME. BE ON THE LOOK OUT. MLPP WE BRINGING THE HEAT.

LOCKED DOWN BY HOOD LOVE 2 COMING IN ONE WEEK!!!!!!

CPSIA information can be obtained
at www.ICGtesting.com
Printed in the USA
LVHW04s1521170918
590425LV00012B/1098/P

9 781718 879485